Man From Blood Creek

Young Matt Doyle had done his time in the notorious Blood Creek prison and he liked to think he had learned his lesson. From now on, it was the straight-and-narrow for him.

No such luck. Not with people like Cash Tyrell and Ace Kelly, not to mention his brutal sidekick Grimm. All were crowding him and wanting to know what his cell-mate Doc Emmet, had told him about a cheap tin watch with the head of a wolf worked into the metal.

These men were ready – and willing – to kill for that information and Doyle found that he would have to brush up on his gun-fighting as well as his trail-herding skills if he wanted to stay alive.

Man From Blood Creek

CLAYTON NASH

A Black Horse Western

ROBERT HALE · LONDON

gw 2529738 4

ISBN 0 7090 7174 4

Robert Hale Limited
Clerkenwell House
Clerkenwell Green
London EC1R 0HT

Typeset by
Derek Doyle & Associates, Liverpool.
Printed and bound in Great Britain by
Antony Rowe Limited, Wiltshire.

1
Freedom

Jigger Bush was waiting for him when they opened the gates of Blood Creek prison and gave him the Jailbird's Farewell – a resounding raspberry from the guards on duty and the confident reminder, '*You'll be ba-a-ack! And we'll be wai-ai-ting!*'

Matt Doyle turned and jammed a thumb against his nose, wiggling his fingers energetically, then, as the guards hurled abuse, turned and walked down the slope to where Jigger Bush lounged in the shade of a clump of trees, slumped on a shaggy blue with another saddled mount, a sorrel, patiently waiting.

'You ain't all that popular, I'd say,' Jigger observed with a crooked grin, leaning out of the saddle and offering his hand to Doyle.

'Thanks for coming, Jigger. Wasn't expecting anybody.'

They gripped hands briefly.

Jigger straightened slowly in the saddle, sobering

5

now, looking down at Doyle. He looked older, thought Bush, a lot older than one year ought to've made him. Still, a year in jail and a year living free – well, there was likely a difference.

Doyle must be – what, now? Twenty-two, twenty-three? Hell, he looked like a man in his thirties, leaned way down so that his crumpled clothes hung on a bony frame. Stooped a mite, too, though still close to six feet, maybe an inch over if he stood straight. Face like a wolf's, mean, hungry, alert, eyes darting around all the time. Voice was a little harsher, yet softer. Hands were calloused, knuckles scarred, and the eyes – hell, those sky-blue eyes that used to twinkle with devilment and recklessness – *Man! They seemed – well – darker, or kind of smoky – and there was no twinkle in them now . . . !*

'They get to you in there, boy?' Jigger asked, no older than Doyle, lean and ropy, but looking better-fed – and there was a go-to-hell look in his eyes that had been there for as long as Doyle had known him.

Doyle lengthened the stirrups on the sorrel and swung aboard with a slow, almost awkward movement, settled in the saddle with a series of uncomfortable shiftings. He glanced at Jigger.

'It was no holiday.'

'Teach you to wear a bandanna next time you hold up a stage!' Jigger laughed, turning his blue. 'Let's ride. The look of that place on the hill makes me depressed.'

Doyle hipped in the saddle and stared back at the grim prison. 'Yeah . . . .'

Bush frowned. 'You sound kinda – regretful!'

'Not really. But I made a couple of good friends in there.'

'Yeah? Hell, way I heard it, a man had to shuffle along with his back to the wall and a sharpened file in both hands, an' don't trust nobody.'

Doyle didn't crack a grin, swivelled his sober eyes to the young outlaw.

'That's about right. Unless you get in with the right group.'

'Oh? You did?'

'Let's just say I found myself some . . . protection.'

Jigger waited, hoping for more, but it seemed Doyle had said all he aimed to say about prison.

'Be thankful you're still riding around free, Jigger.'

'Hell, I am that! Came close to joinin' you once or twice but Ol' Sam come to my rescue.' He slapped the worn butt of the holstered sixgun, saw Doyle's gaze go to the weapon. 'Got a spare one in my saddle-bags for you. But we'll wait'll we get to town, OK?'

Doyle nodded. They rode in silence for a few miles, Jigger starting to speak on several occasions but changing his mind when he got a good look at Doyle's face. The man was miles away, but somehow Bush felt his thoughts were back behind the walls of that damn prison, not running on ahead to the night of hell-raising he had planned.

The town was called – what else? – Blood Creek, and it had lived up to its name ever since Old Jim Bridger himself had given it the tag thirty years or more ago. First there had been a bloody battle with Indians, then, as it became a watering-place for the westbound wagon trains, there were brawls between rival guides and their charges, and, later still, when a town had started to

7

grow, blood had flowed on each occasion.

Now there was law of a kind: a tough, gritty marshal who wore twin sixguns and carried a sawn-off shotgun for good measure, and a slew of handcuffs for the miscreants he gathered in each night and flung in his cellblock behind his office. He earned a portion of each fine imposed by the sour-faced judge and folk knew this was the incentive that kept his cells constantly occupied.

'I don't aim to end up in no cell tonight,' Doyle told Jigger, feeling unbalanced now that he was wearing the sixgun Bush had given him. It had been a long time since he had felt the drag of a Colt on his right hip.

Bush made a placating sign with his hands.

'We'll go easy. Guess the red-eye'll hit you hard. Or was there some rotgut in jail? Heard some of the inmates brew up some hellish stuff.'

'I tried some – once. After the hole in my gut healed up, I swore off it.'

Jigger grinned broadly, laughing, punched Doyle lightly on the shoulder.

'Hey! That's some better, pard! You damn near smiled then!'

Doyle gave him a crooked grin without showing any teeth.

'You don't smile much inside. Guard sees a grin, figures you've been up to some kinda hell. Whether you have or not, you get a going-over with a billy, maybe a few days in The Hole, short rations or a kick in the belly after a full meal, just to remind you that there ain't anything to smile about.'

Jigger sobered. 'Hell, pard, must've been mighty

bad – I'll quit joshin' you about it.'

Doyle hitched at his trousers belt, tugged his old hat down a little on his forehead.

'Can't quite believe it's all behind me. Let's go drown a few sorrows, Jigger!'

Bush let out a wild laugh as they made for the nearest saloon.

'Hell, we'll drown a *lot* of sorrows, a *helluva* lot! And we'll find us a couple sweet-smellin' women who'll let us cradle our poor heads on their soft bosoms and pour out our little hearts to 'em!'

'Sounds good to me!' allowed Doyle as they banged open the batwings and swaggered to the bar, Jigger already calling out,

'Barkeep! Draw two jugs of your foaming ale, my man, and keep 'em comin' as long as we're on our feet. When we're on the floor, why, pour us some of your potent distillation of the sacred rye so that we may regain our upright composure and perhaps find us a couple of beautiful damsels to help support us . . .'

Grinning, Jigger slapped a gold double-eagle on the zinc bar-top and the rugged barman scowled as he slopped beer into a couple of dirty glasses and slammed them down, foam running all over his gnarled hands.

'You keep payin' and I'll bring the beer and the rotgut and even the whores. But you order just one drink and find you can't pay . . .' He showed them the well-worn handle of a knobbly billy that he kept under the counter.

The two young hellers looked at each other, then burst out laughing as they lifted the glasses, touched them in salute and drank deeply.

It was foul and sour and Doyle's belly almost rebelled after the expectations he had built up for his first taste of real beer in a year. But it stayed down and soon had plenty of company.

And it wasn't long before it helped dilute the rotgut whiskey, which was just as well, for it was half-brother to sulphuric acid, and then the singing began and before long some of the other drinkers protested and when told where they could put their unsolicited criticisms, the fists began to fly.

And the glasses and chairs and broken bottles and once it came close to gunfire, but the barkeep's billy broke the wrist of the man who dragged his sixgun and not long afterwards someone yelled 'The marshal's comin'!' and there was a wild scattering of bloody and staggering men and squeals from some of the women who had been watching, as the lawman's boots clumped along the boardwalk.

By the time he crashed open the batwings, scatter-gun held cocked in both hands, there was plenty of wreckage to be seen but only a couple of moaning men lying amidst the splintered furniture and broken glass, and no active combatants. The marshal wasn't fussy. He handcuffed the luckless, barely conscious victims of the brawl and dragged them back to his cell block.

Jigger Bush and Matt Doyle, clothes torn and stained, faces bloody and knuckles split, watched from an upstairs window.

A female voice behind them said, 'Now why don't you boys get outta them dirty clothes and let Merida wash 'em up for you so's you'll have somethin' to wear in the mornin' . . . ?'

They turned back into the room and looked at two barely dressed 'ladies' standing there, hands on ample pink hips, smiling fixed smiles that didn't touch the calculating eyes that looked them over, assessing their wealth and perhaps potential for passing an exciting evening.

Matt Doyle wiped a hand down his bloody face and grinned owlishly as he fumbled at his belt.

'Tol' you I wasn' gonna spend no night in the cells!'

'Last one nekked is a dirty dog!' shouted Jigger, already kicking off his trousers and howling like a coyote in heat as he ran at the squealing, laughing women.

Doyle staggered after him.

There were few smiles the next morning.

Only thundering heads and dry, burning mouths that tasted like something had died there during the night. Not to mention queasy bellies.

And shouted insults and threats as the ladies – known only as Poppy and Pansy – discovered that Jigger didn't have quite as much money as he had thought – or claimed.

The barkeep came, accompanied by his knobbly billy, and two other men who might have been his brothers, both carrying kinfolk of the infamous billy wielded by the barkeep.

It was not a time for talking and Jigger Bush found out that Matt Doyle hadn't forgotten their old routine for use on such occasions . . . .

It involved grabbing the swearing, admonishing whores, holding them in front as the men advanced with raised batons, then charging forward as they continued screaming, straight at the menacing men. Startled, not wanting to damage their womenfolk, the men naturally retreated, cramped for space in the room, jostling each other as they tried to back out of the doorway. The women kept on screaming and struggling, then they were thrust after the men, tripping over them, the whole kit-and-caboodle ending up in a thrashing heap in the passage as Jigger and Doyle, half-dressed, grabbing their clothes that the Mexican servant had washed and ironed during the night, and – the final stage of the manoeuvre – leapt over the struggling group and *ran like hell*.

They cleared town more or less dressed, riding their mounts bareback, having to leave their saddle gear when the unpaid livery man reached for his hayfork. They passed the marshal standing in the doorway of his office, and he sent them on their way with a burst from his scattergun into the air as they thundered over the wooden bridge across the creek and headed for the hills . . . .

By noon they were far enough away to stop and dredge up a laugh or two, but Jigger Bush's laugh died like a man struck down by apoplexy, when he said,

'Matt, you ain't changed a bit! Thought at first you had, but you ain't, I'm glad to say! You're still a top hand at hell-raisin' . . . Man, I've got us a little ol' bank in Wildwood lined up, and a stage outta the mines in the Anvil Breaks that'll give us a month of wild nights in —'

'Not me, Jigger.'

Bush blinked at Doyle's interruption. 'What . . .?'

'No more jobs, Jigger – I've learned my lesson. It's hard graft for me from now on. A straight job or I ain't interested . . . So looks like we've come to the parting of the ways, you and me . . . .'

'You gotta be joshin'!'

Matt Doyle merely stared back with those once-blue eyes that seemed to have taken on some of the grey doom of the prison yard.

Jigger Bush writhed in the saddle, spitting angrily.

'Oh, *goddammit*! You ain't!'

2
Many Trails

As Matt Doyle spat, he felt as if he had hawked up half the Mississippi. The dust in the holding corrals at St Louis was thicker than smoke in a Colorado forest fire and the grit had worked up his nostrils and into his ears and eyes, crunched between his teeth. It had plastered against the sweat of his shirt collar and rubbed the back of his neck raw, despite his bandanna. He figured if he climbed out of the saddle and shook himself like a dog he would disappear into the roiling dust background, never to be seen again.

But that wasn't a good idea – not on pay-day. He aimed to be head of the line when Big Robbie Macleay doled out the trail pay. It had been a rough nine weeks on the trail up from the Red River and there was to be a fighting bonus added because of the raid by Indians, and an attempt to steal the whole damn herd by a large bunch of rustlers.

A few of them wouldn't be rustling any more and some of the Indians had gone to their Happy Hunting Grounds. Some of the trail crew, too – like Curly

Hopgood, a young wrangler who had caught an arrow through the neck, died in Doyle's arms with his eyes wide open, wondering what had happened to him, trying to speak, but the words drowned in blood.

But Doyle didn't want to think about that; he had liked Curly and they had thrown one memorable wingding together in a Kansas trail-town. No more, though – which just went to show that a man could bust a gut trying to stay on the straight and narrow and still have his life cut short.

Well, he had sent Curly's things to the sister he had spoken about in Denver, carved his name on a wooden cross set on a lonely trailside grave, and that was about it.

A man never knew what was waiting for him – Old Dan Emmett in the jail had said that many a time, but Dan was old, serving a twenty-year sentence for some kind of killing and, with thirty years separating them, Doyle had figured he had *his* future all planned. Not in a lot of detail, but he had learned his lesson about breaking the law – and getting caught. Old Dan had told him the only sure way *not* to get caught was in not breaking the law in the first place.

Made sense to Doyle after what he'd seen in prison. He swore he wasn't about to go through that experience again, knew he'd be loco not to gain something from it.

Of course, Jigger Bush, that day – must be nigh on two years ago now: *Hell, time sure can fly!* – yeah, well Jigger had scoffed at his resolution to go straight.

'You won't last three months, Matt, old son! Go ahead, ride on out now, forget them easy jobs I got lined up – I can always find someone else to help me out. But you make a deal with me: meet me in – say, Laredo – three months from now and if you're still goin' straight, I'll buy the drinks and pay for the women and we'll have one helluva time and afterwards – I'll damn well join you!' He had paused and grinned. 'But I know I'm safe! You'll have cut away on a side trail and done somethin' agin the law by then . . . .'

They had shaken hands on it, but three months came and went and by the time Doyle realized he hadn't kept the rendezvous, he had been trapping mustangs on the Wind River for a stageline, a long way from Laredo.

Jigger more than likely hadn't kept the appointment, anyway. They had parted still friends, but Jigger Bush hadn't been pleased about Doyle's decision.

Well, that was a long time ago now and he'd only seen Jigger once. A few weeks back, actually, when he was riding nighthawk at the herd's river camp by the salt fork of the San Pedro. This rider had come silently out of the darkness after Doyle had settled down some restless steers with a few verses of a smutty trail-song and whispered his name, causing Doyle to nearly jump out of the saddle, reaching for his sixgun.

The click of a gun hammer cocking checked his move.

'Relax, Mr Goody – it's only me: Jigger.'

Doyle was stunned, didn't speak. Then he heard the soft unmistakable chuckle and knew it was indeed Jigger Bush.

'Still workin' hard graft after all this time! Hey, you never showed in Laredo and, you know, I even checked out a couple jails to see if you was in one! But you weren't.'

Doyle drew down a long breath.

'What you want, Jigger?'

'Ahh! Figured it might be like that. All puffed up with livin' honest, huh?' Doyle heard him spit. 'If you can call it livin'!'

'I enjoy it. Specially not havin' to dodge the local law at every town and getting a crick in the neck from looking over my shoulder every trail I ride.'

'Sounds mighty borin' to me. Hey, you got enough to pay your share of that night in Blood Crick? You never did cough up.'

Doyle was silent a moment. 'Never figured I had to. It was always whichever one of us had the money paid – the other feller's turn next time.'

'Well, this *is* next time so cough up fifty bucks.'

'You're loco! You never spent that much for one thing and that's almost all my trail pay.'

'See what I mean? You're leadin' a miserable life – for pennies!'

'I ain't the one putting the bite on a pard for a handout.'

'Judas, you *have* developed into a smug son of a bitch!' There was a slight movement across the stars and Doyle knew Jigger had leaned towards him. 'This ain't a handout, you goddamn saddle bum! You *owe* me and I aim to collect – one way or another.'

Doyle remained silent for a space and then said:

'Now we're getting to it, ain't we? You knew damn

17

well I wouldn't have any fifty bucks on me. But you got something else figured, right?'

It was Jigger's turn to remain silent for a spell.

'You ain't forgot *all* the old ways, I see. Well, yeah, now you mention it, if you can't come up with the fifty bucks, mebbe you can square things – another way.'

'Like what?'

'Look around you. Nigh on two thousand cows dreamin' away. You arrange to do nighthawk when the herd reaches Bagnell's Pass and that's all you got to do. Sure, you'll have a small knot on your head when you wake up but that'll make it look good for you with Big Robbie . . . OK?'

'No.'

Jigger sighed. 'Well, I guess I expected that. But if you don't, could be Big Robbie'll get to hear about your time spent in Blood Creek prison . . . . You'd be out of a job then and I can't guarantee I could take you back into the gang.'

'Wouldn't want to come, Jigger – I like this kind of life. I'm never gonna grow rich, I guess, but I get along OK and one day I'll have my own small spread or horse-breaking outfit – I'll get by. Matter of fact, Big Robbie thinks I've got ambition for a trail hand. Most of 'em don't think beyond the next town and how many drinks they can put away.'

Jigger was silent yet again, then spat.

'You – you're sayin' Big Robbie *knows* about Blood Creek? I don't b'lieve it!'

'Believe it, Jigger. But I gotta say I don't give a good goddamn one way or the other.'

'You lousy . . . ! After all them years we rode

together! After I met you comin' outta the prison gate . . . Why you son of a . . .'

Doyle rammed home his spurs, jumping his horse into Jigger, knocking the man out of the saddle. He leaned down, making sure Bush heard his gun hammer cock.

'Shut up, Jigger!' he hissed. 'You'll spook the herd. Now get the hell away from me. I've told every outfit I've worked for, candidly, about my past. Sometimes, they've sent me on my way, didn't want to know me, sometimes they took a chance and hired me. When they do that, I ride for the brand. But, you're right – I do owe you something after all the years we rode together. So I'm not gonna drag you down to the trail camp, but if there's any attempt to stampede or rustle this herd between here and St Louis, I'll see your name on a wanted dodger. I'd just as soon part friends, but that's up to you now.'

Bush was on his feet and after a while Doyle saw him holster his sixgun.

'OK, Matt – that's the way you want it, that's the way it's gonna be. *Not* partin' friends, I don't mean that. We cain't be friends ever again, but we ever cross trails, I reckon I'm gonna kill you.'

'You shouldn't've told me, Jigger. Now I'll be expecting it.'

'You do *just* that! Expect it – 'cause it'll happen, all right.' He paused to snigger and there was amusement in his voice as he added, 'Bet your life on it!'

Then he was gone, leading his horse.

Doyle had been edgy for the rest of the drive but they had arrived in St Louis with only the expected trail troubles with a herd that size. Soon, after washing-up, when the steers were divided amongst the holding pens and the buyers were inspecting them, Doyle forgot about Jigger Bush, collected his pay, and hit the high spots with the rest of the crew, but he left half his money with Big Robbie to bank for him in the small account he had started a few months earlier. There wasn't much in it yet, but one day there'd be enough for a quarter-section, somewhere along the Wind River if he could manage it, but maybe somewhere else. Didn't matter – as long as it was his . . . .

So he went into town happy with the rest of the off duty crew, aiming to have himself a high old time.

And he almost made it.

He was making real progress with a young bar girl who had most of Big Robbie's crew moving in on her, when he heard a name that stopped the sweet-sounding words dead on his lips.

'Cash Tyrell!' the saloon-owner greeted a trail-dusty man who had just slouched through the batwings and was making his way towards the bar. 'Well, smoke me! I ain't seen you in a coon's age – 'Fact, *two* coons' ages!'

The newcomer looked at the saloon-man in his broadcloth frock-coat and flowered vest, frowned briefly, and then a grin split through the layer of trail dirt.

'That you, Ace Kelly?' They moved towards each other and gripped hands, pumping arms energetically as each tried to outdo the other. 'You son of a gun, you've come up in the world! Guess no one caught you dealin' from the bottom of the deck, huh?'

'Only man who did is long dead!' Kelly grinned, standing back and looking at the trail man. 'Hell, you don't just need a bath, you oughta jump in the river, *then* take a bath!'

'Dirt of three states there,' Tyrell said, slapping at his clothes with his battered hat, raising a cloud of dust that brought exaggerated coughing from the saloon-man. 'One bein' the sovereign state of the Lone Star, so place your right hand over your heart and bend the knee, you goddamn card-sharp!'

Just for a moment the saloon-man's face straightened and then the grin returned and he slapped Tyrell on the back.

'Enough insults! Come on up to my rooms. You can have a bath there and I'll have one of my gals scrub your back – or whatever – if you want, while you swig from a jug of my best whiskey . . .'

'Leave the gal till later – I've had a hankerin' to hug a jug of decent redeye for nigh on a thousand miles.'

'Then you come to the right place.'

The pair of them headed up the stairs, talking animatedly, and the young girl pushed Doyle's shoulder roughly.

'Hey! I'm still here, you know!'

'Huh? Oh, sorry, darlin' – I – I've got a sudden headache.'

'Headache!'

He smiled crookedly and pushed a ten-dollar coin into her low-cut bodice. 'Don't lose the place – I'll be along a little later.'

The money placated her hurt feelings but within minutes she was laughing and tussling with another trail man. Doyle didn't notice or didn't care: he was intent on going up the stairs after Kelly and Cash Tyrell.

He wished his head was clearer but figured he could manage what he wanted to do. He flattened against one end of the passageway, peering around briefly, seeing the two men enter the door at the far end, close to the exit that led to an outside stairway.

Doyle waited, willing his steaming brain to settle down, feeling the sobriety gradually taking hold; luckily he hadn't taken much liquor on board, mostly beer with only a couple of whiskeys – it was too much like rotgut for him. Anyway, Robbie Macleay wanted him to cut the best horses out of the remuda first thing, aiming to sell them.

There was muted laughter from down the passage, a couple of doors opened and closed. A woman squealed. A man laughed harshly and another cursed. He heard the door leading to the outside stairs open and close, two men arguing, their voices hacked to silence when the door swung shut. By now he was sitting on the floor, back against the passage wall, hat on crooked, slack-jawed, muttering a little, grinning at nothing.

The men who came swaying up the stairs from the bar room with their frails, making for one of the many dingy rooms that opened off the hallway, glanced at him without interest. Just another drunk who thought he was more of a stallion than he was . . . .

Then there came a period of reasonable quiet and fewer men and women using the stairs. Doyle stood up, straightened his hat, loosened his sixgun in his holster and made his way along to the door that Kelly and

Tyrell had used.

He pushed his hat to the back of his head, sweat-matted fair hair curling on to his forehead as he turned side on, placing an ear to the panelling. He was facing down the passage so he would see anyone coming up from the bar room. Muted voices reached him through the varnished panelling, and he also heard water splashing, male laughter.

'. . . man-and-a-dog spread, just outside of Joplin.' That must be Tyrell, his Texas drawl very different from Ace Kelly's Carolina swampwater speech.

'Missouri?' Kelly said, sounding surprised. 'You drove a herd of two hundred beeves clear across the state to the meat-market here?'

'Hired me a couple grubliners, paid 'em twenny bucks apiece – yeah, this is where the best prices are, Ace, and I got me a good wad. Figure you can stand my company for a week or so?'

'Hell, yeah! Stay here with me, in these rooms. Everythin' you want is laid on – you won't even have to get outta bed 'less you want to.'

Tyrell laughed. 'I'm hopin' I won't be *able* to!'

Kelly joined in the laughter. 'Well, I know just the gal who can help you there. But I never thought I'd see the day you'd settle down, not Cash Tyrell, scourge of the Mississippi river-boats!'

'Made a killin'. Couple of greenhorns with silver-plated wallets figured it meant they could show us locals how poker was *really* played. Made two of us rich and one of them greenhorns went up on deck and blew his brains out.'

'Get away!'

'Gospel – 'fraid of goin' home to face Pappy or somethin'. Other reckoned he was cheated but somehow he fell overboard and we never did hear any more about it . . .'

Kelly guffawed. 'You are one cool son of a bitch, Cash, old pard. Lemme get you another bottle and then I'll send in The Claw to scrub your back.'

'*The Claw?*'

'She likes to leave her mark on the men she pleasures – someplace it don't show.'

'Hey! I dunno about that . . .'

Kelly could hardly speak for laughing. 'You oughta see your face! It . . .'

He spun around angrily as he heard the door open. 'The hell don't you knock?' he snarled at one of his bouncers who stepped to one side and dragged in one of the trail men Kelly had seen drinking downstairs, trying to make time with young Judy the Nudie.

'I come up the side stairs an' found him with his ear pressed to your door, boss,' growled the bouncer, big and wide, with a battered face that had been kissed by too many fists and empty bottles – maybe a couple of full ones, too.

Tyrell wiped soap out of his eyes and squinted as Kelly walked across, his body half-screening the apparently drunken cowboy.

'What the hell you think you're up to?' Kelly snapped.

Matt Doyle seemed to have trouble focusing and standing upright. The bouncer shook him, swearing at him.

'Hey, *that* ain't Libby!' Matt poin ed limply at Tyrell

24

sitting in the hip-bath, looked around the big carpeted and richly curtained room. 'Libby! Hey, Libby! You said to meet you up here and here I am! Where you? Where's Libby, mister?'

Kelly scowled, glanced at the bouncer and jerked his head. 'Throw him out – better see he knows better'n to come prowling around the private section again.'

'Right, boss.' The bouncer tightened his grip on Doyle and dragged him out into the passage. 'Sorry I forgot to knock, boss.'

Kelly grunted, pushed both men out and closed the door. He grinned at Tyrell. 'Wouldn't want his head in the mornin'.'

Tyrell looked at his empty glass. 'Well, I'm tryin' for my own special kinda mornin' head . . . if you don't mind?'

Kelly laughed and walked to the sideboy where the bottles of booze glinted in the lamplight.

Out on the landing at the head of the outside stairs, the bouncer thrust the still-acting Doyle hard against the wall.

'You might've of fooled the boss, but you din' fool me, you lousy trail bum! You was lookin' for an empty room to get in and rob, weren't you . . . ?'

'You got it wrong, pardner . . .'

Doyle grunted as the big man smashed his head back against the clapboards and the world burst into a shower of stars. He felt the man's thick fingers working through his pockets but his legs were weak and his arms flailed uselessly as the bouncer took all his remaining money.

Just as his head began to clear and he managed to bunch up a hard right fist, the bouncer threw him down the stairs. Doyle clattered and bounced and somersaulted all the way to the bottom. He sprawled, dazed, blood trickling into one eye. The stairs shook as the bouncer came clumping down, thrusting Doyle's money into his shirt pocket. The cowboy made two attempts to get to his feet but was too slow and groggy. The bouncer reached the bottom and swung a big boot into the cowboy's side, sending him staggering into the alley.

Doyle was hurt, gasping, held his side and turned his head towards the bouncer as he closed in, ready to beat him some more. Doyle's boot touched an empty bottle and he reached down for it but the bouncer kicked him again and knocked him flailing into some untidily stacked crates. As Doyle fell, the bouncer grinned tightly.

'I'm gonna kick your sorry butt all the way down Main, you sneaky son of a bitch!'

Then he suddenly howled as Doyle, his hand wrapped around the neck of the empty bottle, smashed it into his shin. The bouncer bent down quickly, hopping on one leg. Doyle got to his feet groggily, bounced the bottle off the man's head, swung again and managed to smash it this time. The bouncer fell to his knees, blood pouring into his eyes. Doyle kneed him in the face and started to reach for the man's shirt pocket to recover his money.

Kneeling, he turned quickly as the door at the head of the stairs opened and spilled lamplight showed him two more bouncers. They shouted at him and came charging down the stairs.

Doubled over, hugging his aching ribs, Doyle lunged his way down the alley, towards Main, leaving his money behind.

3
Caught!

It must have been one of the wettest Septembers Missouri had ever known. Day after day the sky clouded up, leaden and black, and the lightning seared and the rain spilled out like a million buckets had been up-ended all at once.

Doyle was trapped for two days in a canyon that had been dry when he had started through but now looked like a small lake, swirling brown water meshed with tree tops and dead animals driving him way up the sloping sides. He climbed a tree after turning his mount loose, figuring it had enough sense to find a dry place. There was a snake in the same tree and he finished up shooting its head off, snared the limp body before it could fall and ate it raw. It wasn't all that bad and actually helped slake his thirst.

Kind of crazy, he reckoned, trapped in a flood and dying of thirst at the same time. But he was afraid to drink the flood waters with so many dead animals floating in it and lots of silt, too.

His tobacco was damp but he managed to coax a

cigarette alight and drew the smoke deep into his lungs. He shivered as he coughed, hugged himself as he smoked and thought about the last two days . . . .

He had managed to give the vengeful bouncers the slip in St Louis, had tracked down Big Robbie at the Regal Hotel where he was doing some sort of deal with two meathouse buyers. He caught the trail boss's eye and the big man excused himself, came over to the door, took Doyle's arm and led him on to the hotel porch.

'The hell's happened to you?'

'Long story, Robbie, but I got thrown down some stairs and rolled for my cash. I need that money I left with you.'

'For your ranch, you said. You don't want it now, boy, just gonna blow it on more booze and women and you'll have nothin' to show for it but a hangover – or mebbe somethin' even more unpleasant to remind you of this night.'

Doyle was shaking his throbbing head all the time Macleay was talking.

'Robbie! I need that dough – I'm sorry. I won't be able to work the remuda for you. I gotta quit town tonight.'

The sandy-haired trail boss frowned, genuinely concerned, a father-figure with sons of his own.

'Listen, son, if you're in real trouble, tell me about it and I'll —'

'No, no. No trouble. I – I've just got to get out of town and back to Joplin, Missouri, soon as I can.'

'Joplin? Well, I sure do know some prettier places than that! Matt, I've been straight with you because you were straight with me about your jail time, but if anything's come up I can help you with . . .'

Doyle was edgy now, hurting, losing patience.

'For Chrissakes, just gimme my goddamn money, will you?'

He saw the hurt flare in Big Robbie's glare-shot eyes, still watering from the long drive. Then the old man's lips tightened and he dug his hand into his pocket and began counting out some bills. Without looking up, he said:

'You wait till mornin', I'll have worked out how much the bonus is gonna be . . .'

'Split mine amongst the boys. Kinda – compensation for walking out on you like this.'

Macleay handed across some folded money and Doyle met his gaze, blinking away a little blood from a wound above his right eye. After a little more hesitation, Robbie thrust out his right hand and they gripped.

'Whatever you've got in mind, boy, I hope it works out for you. And, should there be anythin' I can do for you sometime, you know where the ranch is.'

Doyle felt miserable and seemed to shrink in on himself as he nodded, put the money away and then limped off into the night, trying to remember where he had left his horse.

Now, up in the tree with the water lapping his feet, daylight fast fading, what there was of it, and the rain refusing to let up, Matt Doyle wondered just what the hell he was doing here.

He knew *why* he had come but it had been an

impulse and now it was wearing thin and he wasn't even sure about this. But it was a debt in a way, and he always paid his debts. Maybe he was stupid doing it like this but – well, hell, he had learned a lot of stuff in Blood Creek prison and while much of it was trash, Dan 'Doc' Emmett had steered him in the right direction about many things.

One of them was, work out who your true friends are then never let them down, stay in touch and if they need help, even if they don't ask for it, don't stint in the giving – even if you have to risk your own neck.

That's what he was doing now, but he was beholden and this chance had come his way to help pay back part of what he owed, so he remembered Emmett's lesson and aimed to follow through, come hell or high water.

He chuckled. High water was right.

The hell might come later – after he got to Joplin. If he ever did.

But he arrived late the following day. The rain stopped as suddenly as it had begun, and he was surprised at how quickly the flood waters drained away.

He didn't even have to go looking for his horse; it came whinnying down the slope, muddy, the saddle slung under its belly, the bridle somehow tangled in the lower jaw.

It took little work to get things fixed and, though his belly was growling with hunger, all his supplies spoiled, he rode along the muddy trail happily enough, seeing the town slowly rising out of the west a couple of hours before sundown.

It was just on dark when he rode in and found a cheap room for the night.

Before he turned in he had learned where Cash Tyrell's spread was and set out just after daylight.

He didn't care for the country much, nor the people come to that. Missourians tended to treat strangers with suspicion, no doubt a hangover from the war years when a man wasn't even sure which side his brother was fighting on. The ranch was in a small basin and pretty much isolated, as he had learned in the saloon last night – which suited him fine.

There appeared to have been some flood-damage, flattened grass and weeds and scattered gear as well as a collapsed barn marking the trail of raging water tearing down from the high slopes. The house appeared to be OK, a longish building of logs, solid-looking, with a riverstone fireplace. No smoke trickled from the chimney. Which also suited him.

He stayed back in a clump of trees, watching. Two men were clearing away debris from the barn, muddy, stopping now and again to hurl a few clods at each other, having a time of it. Which told him the boss – Cash Tyrell – had not yet returned from St Louis.

Doyle had been a mite concerned that the rancher might have gotten back before him by a shorter trail, seeing as he had been treed by the rain for a couple of days. He waited a spell but could not see any more ranch hands. To be sure, he rode around the spread, remembering Tyrell had told Kelly it was only a quarter-section. He found a herd in good grassland that was naturally fenced in by the rise and fall of the land and a creek that now boiled from the rain but would be permanent water normally. There were about a hundred head, he figured, fattening up for next season.

Tyrell's prime herd . . . .

'Well, could be they're gonna lose some of that fat even before they've got it on,' he murmured to himself, took his Colt from his holster and rode down amongst them, shooting and yelling. They would hear it from the house but that was OK – he aimed to be long gone by the time they got here and then they'd be busy rounding up the herd – it ought to be scattered to hell and gone by then.

The steers were spooky, no doubt because of the recent rain, and it took only one cylinder of cartridges to bunch them up and set them charging for the low land between the hills. He reloaded, made sure they headed for the muddy flats and then pulled back into timber, watching as the steers bawled and thundered and began to scatter as they hit open country.

When he saw the two frantic ranch hands riding down – bareback, so it seemed they had leapt on their mounts in a mighty hurry – he smiled thinly, hauled his mount around and headed back towards the house.

Nothing was locked up so he tied his horse to a juniper and went inside. There was nothing remarkable about the ranch house: he had seen hundreds like it over the years. This one obviously was male-only habitation and he found a back room with two untidy, smelly bunks in it as well as muddy workboots and clothing that hadn't been washed since Gettysburg, he judged.

The two ranch hands, he allowed, having noticed there was no bunkhouse.

The other bedroom was a little neater and cleaner and had solid handmade furniture, clothes' closet, a side-table and another along one wall with cupboards.

He pushed his hat to the back of his head, aware that his heart was hammering and bouncing against his ribs. It had been a long time since he had broken into any kind of ranch house or store or office with the intention of stealing.

He was once again breaking the law!

He acknowledged that to himself, but there were what Doc Emmett had called 'extenuating circumstances'. Doc was good with words, good enough after years of study in the prison library to conduct his own appeal against his sentence: he was not only fighting to have it reduced, he wanted a full pardon and his name cleared.

Anyway, Doc was a strange man in many ways, not big physically, several inches shorter than Doyle and thirty pounds lighter, but when that bunch had cornered him in the washhouse, Doc had come wading in, laying about him with fists and a heavy workboot. The five convicts went down one by one, battered and bloody, but Doc didn't leave it there. He used the steel-shod heel of that boot to give the moaning men such a working-over that they were forever afterwards affected by it and the whole cell block benefited.

'This boy is off-limits to you scum,' Doc told them in that easy, mellow voice, breathing a little hard as the bloody convicts rolled and writhed and groaned. He kicked a couple to make sure he had their attention. 'You hear? Doyle is under my protection. If you, if *anyone*, tries for him again, they'll die in here and it won't be pleasant.'

Then while the dread words still hung in the steam-

34

ing washhouse, the other naked, soaped-up cons watching silently, Emmett grinned and moved towards Doyle, who had taken two blows in the mouth before Doc had started swinging. The older man's grin widened when Doyle backed his naked buttocks against the zinc-lined wall and snatched up one of the cakes of hard lye soap the prison provided.

'I'll screw this into your eyes you come near me!' Doyle threatened, stopping Emmett. 'I'm obliged for what you done, but if you think you can take up what they was trying to start, you'll end up blinded and maybe with mangled *cojones* as well!'

Doc had laughed, spread his arms.

'Relax, boy, I'm not that way inclined. I just thought it was about time I spiked the guns – if you'll pardon the pun – of these gentlemen on the floor. You finish your wash and I'll see you outside.'

Matt Doyle was mighty surprised when Doc Emmett kept his word; he never tried to molest Doyle in all the months they shared a cell, somehow arranged by Emmett, who seemed to be popular with guards, most prisoners *and* the warden.

That was when he learned that the man he knew as Doc Emmett had a daughter in the outside world.

'Ain't seen her in years but she's mine and I'd like to think that someone might step in if ever she got in a bad situation and needed help while I'm not around.'

To this day, Doyle wasn't exactly sure why Emmett had taken a shine to him, but it had sure helped him through the brutal time he served in Blood Creek. And the old man had taken to confiding in Doyle: not long before he had been released, Doc had told him about a man named Cash Tyrell, where'bouts unknown, but one who had changed Emmett's life – for the worse.

'If ever you come across that son of a bitch, Matt, I'd be obliged if you'd bust his snoot for him and kick his teeth in on my behalf and if you can, strip him of all he owns, like he done to me, give him a taste of being down and out and so an easy target for those who want to do you harm.'

Emmett seemed to have been unusually upset by this Tyrell.

Doyle had never forgotten the name and now he had his chance to do something for Doc Emmett. So far he hadn't done anything but stampede Tyrell's herd; he was almost certain the man was the one Doc had spoken about, but he aimed to make sure before he completed his hastily composed plan. He knew what he had to do.

He tore the bedroom apart. Slashed the mattress, ripped out shelving in the cupboards, tapped the walls for hollow hiding-places. He found a small poke of money, less than fifty dollars, a single double-eagle amongst the coins. There were some papers relating to the ranch, title deeds, prove-up conditions and so on. The dates seemed right, just after the time Emmett claimed Tyrell had wrecked his life.

But he didn't find what he was looking for.

He stood in the centre of the room, staring at the mess he had made, but he didn't feel much guilt, for he was sure in his own mind he had the right man. He just wanted to be *certain*-sure before he burned down the house and barn and ran off the remuda . . . .

He kicked aside some of the mess, including a hammer he had used to tear out the shelves. The rust-spotted head thudded down from the pile of rubbish and when it hit the floorboards there was a hollow sound.

In minutes he had the hidey-hole opened up and pulled out the small metal box with the padlock on it. He grinned tightly: if he was going to find what he had come for, this was the place to look. He set down the box, held it steady with his left hand and bashed at the padlock and hasp with the hammer. The lot broke away, twisting the metal rim of the lid a little. Doyle grinned expectantly as he reached to work the lid open.

'You thievin' bastard!'

He was squatting on his hams and spun so fast towards the voice that he almost lost balance. He saw Tyrell, mud-spattered from a hard ride, pulling his sixgun from his holster as he stood in the doorway.

Doyle didn't hesitate: he flung the hammer and it struck Tyrell in the shoulder, bringing a grunt of pain from the man, wrenching him around so that the sixgun fell from his numbed fingers. He grabbed at his useless arm, face twisted in agony, but still tried to thrust off the wall.

Doyle was already moving, swung a fist that took Tyrell on the jaw and knocked him to one knee. The man shook his head and Doyle grabbed his dirty shirt collar and threw him on the floor.

'Stay put!' he snapped, right hand closing about his gun butt. 'You made good time from St Louis, considering all that rain.'

Tyrell squinted up through his pain. 'Hey! You're that drunk who was lookin' for some whore in Ace Kelly's!' Then he sobered. 'Or *were* you drunk, you son of a bitch!'

'Not quite as bad as I made out.'

'Well what the hell you doin' here? Aaaah, I can *see* what you're doin'! You're stealin' my money! Why, damnit?'

His eyes went to the metal box rather than the poke of coins Doyle had left on one end of the side-table.

'Just like you stole from Doc Emmett.'

Tyrell blinked. 'Who?'

Doyle kicked him in the side. 'Don't play dumb with me! You know who I mean! Dan Emmett!'

Tyrell slowly shook his head and Doyle felt a tightening in his stomach. *Judas, had he made a mistake? This man's puzzlement seemed genuine . . .*

'I dunno any Emmett, Dan, Doc or Daisy Mae. You plumb loco, son?'

Doyle took in a deep breath. 'You were pards with Emmett in some deal that he didn't go into detail about. You were close to pulling it off, then you up and run – with all his money, everything he had – and, likely, set him up to be charged with murder and sent to Blood Creek for twenty years.'

Tyrell's face was grey now – from the pain? Or Doyle's words?

'I dunno what you're talkin' about! I tell you I don't *know* any Emmett! You've made a mistake, boy! Look, leave my stuff and get outta here and you'll hear no more about it.'

Doyle was confused. He shook his head slowly.

'You fit the man who done Emmett wrong. Name, age, description, the date on the deeds to this place.' He dropped his gaze to the mangled tin box. 'And I reckon if I open that, I'll find the last bit of evidence to prove you are the right Cash Tyrell.'

'Get outta here while you can, boy! You dunno how lucky you are, me givin' you the chance to save your neck.'

Doyle smiled coldly, picked up the metal box. Tyrell stiffened.

'Leave that!'

'Uh-uh. What I want is in here, pretty sure about that. If it is – I'll be back and I'll burn your damn ranch down around your ears, run your prime herd off a cliff, and maybe even put a bullet in you if I see you.'

'Christ! Just what the hell do you owe this Emmett?'

'Scum like you wouldn't savvy. No, I think I'll take the time to open this right now and square things while I'm here. I sure don't aim to have you set the law on me and take the chance of going back to Blood Creek.'

'Hah! An ex-con! Judas priest!'

Doyle kicked him under the jaw just as he heard riders outside and a voice called:

'Boss! Boss! We've had a stampede and half the herd's bogged down . . .'

Doyle headed for the door and the man must have heard him for he said:

'Thought I seen you ride in, so I . . .'

He saw it wasn't Tyrell coming out and he reached for his gun.

Doyle raised his Colt, yelling, 'Don't!'

But he hadn't seen the second ranch hand off to his

right. First he knew about it was when the bullet bit a handful of splinters from the door frame and sent him ducking wildly as they cut into the side of his face and one ear.

Doyle stumbled onto the porch and both men fired at him, their prancing, mud-stained horses causing them to miss. Doyle dived for the floorboards, triggering at the man dead ahead first, rolling and shooting at the one on his right.

The horse of the one dead ahead reared with a whinny, and Doyle saw the red slash across the neck left by his bullet. The rider fell awkwardly out of the saddle, lay twisted on the ground, dazed, his gun a couple of feet away now. The man on the right crouched low in his saddle and spurred his mount across the yard, trying to ride up onto the porch. Doyle leapt up to the rail, dived headlong at the man and carried him out of the saddle. They hit hard and mud sprayed as they rolled, knees and fists going, guns clubbed. Doyle took a glancing blow that knocked his hat off and swung his gun back-handed in a reflex action. It took the cowboy across the temple and the man dropped, out cold.

As Doyle rolled to his feet, the other man had found his gun and lifted it in both hands, squinting through the mud as he fired in Doyle's direction. The bullet fanned his face and he fired his last shot into the man's left leg. The cowhand howled and writhed, all the fight gone out of him now.

Matt Doyle scooped up the metal box, looked around for his hat, but then Tyrell staggered through the doorway, shooting wildly. Doyle skidded, changed direction, ran around the side of the house and sprinted for the juniper where his horse waited.

Wild bullets were still buzzing around him as he hit leather and got the hell out of there.

4
Gamble

The lid of the metal box had become jammed when a blow from the hammer had skidded off the padlock hasp and bent the rim. Now, a long way from Tyrell's place, crouched over a small fire in a high camp, Doyle tried to open it.

He broke a horny thumbnail and cut one finger, swearing, for even a small cut on a cowboy's hand could become a nuisance, which was why most cowpokes wore workgloves. He tried his hunting-knife next and turned the air blue when the tip of the blade broke off. Stubborn now, he tipped the box upside down, feeling a transfer of weight inside although the sound was muted, and hammered at the bent rim with the butt of his sixgun. After splintering the edge of the cedar butt-plate, the lid finally flew open and the contents spilled onto the saddle cloth he had spread out.

The biggest item was bulky and wrapped in a square of felt. He set it to one side, knowing full well what it must be. The other things were mainly papers; he found Cash Tyrell's birth certificate, some ink-faded letters from his mother written several years ago, a badly spelled note from a sister berating him for not being at their mother's bedside when she died. There was a sepia, dog-eared postcard of a youngish woman in a 'naughty' pose, apparently naked beneath what looked like a length of curtain draped diagonally across her puppy-fat body. There was a necklace of cheap china beads, a lock of hair wrapped in a section of a page torn from the Tombstone *Epitaph*, and, of all things, a man's molar with a gigantic decay hole in one side.

'Now that's taking sentimentality just a mite too far, I reckon,' murmured Doyle, picking up the felt package and beginning to unwrap it.

It wasn't large and in half a minute he held the object in his hands. He nodded. Just as he figured. Tyrell was the one who had betrayed Doc Emmett, all right.

What had been wrapped carefully in the felt square was a gold – or gold-plated – pocket-watch, ornately decorated on the front lid with the raised figure of a wolf howling at the moon and, on the back, an intricate design of intertwined acanthus leaves surrounding an embossed head of a wolf.

The man Doc Emmett had supposedly murdered was named Thomas Resnick, partner in a meat-packing house, and, the law claimed, he had owned just such a watch as this.

According to the prosecuting attorney, Doc had taken it from Resnik's body. Doc Emmett told Doyle that while he hadn't killed Resnik, he *had* taken the watch and, later, his one-time partner and sometime 'friend', Cash Tyrell, had stolen it from *him*, as well as other items. But he hadn't mentioned this in court because Tyrell had disappeared with all the agency's money and the books that showed it was making a reasonable profit. The law claimed Emmett's motive for killing Resnik was the theft of a large sum of money because Dcc was broke, so, unable to prove different because of Tyrell's absconding, this only further damaged his case. Unpaid bills for feed, transport and rent on holding-pens made the whole deal look mighty bad for Emmett . . . .

That had been Doc's story, anyway.

He'd told it fluently, confidently, persuasively, with all the details ready to hand and Doyle believed him.

Emmett was lucky he hadn't been hanged. The judge – and jury – thought there was some cause for at least a little doubt about his guilt and he was sentenced to twenty years hard in Blood Creek instead of the hangman's noose.

While Emmett didn't go so far as to say Tyrell had killed Resnik – who had, incidentally, been dealing with Tyrell exclusively, something else Doc had been unable to prove – he figured there had to be some reason why Tyrell had wanted that watch. It wouldn't help Emmett's appeal now, even if Doyle took it to the law, which he didn't aim to do, for he was already in a heap of trouble after what he had done to Tyrell and he would have trouble explaining how *he* had come by the watch. The best way Emmett could be helped was for Tyrell to admit to the killing. Which he wouldn't do, of course.

Not voluntarily, leastways.

But for now, Doyle had to clear this country if he aimed to stay free. Tyrell would likely set the law on him and he had been warned by the judge at his trial, that if he came before him again, he would get a minimum of ten years . . .

He couldn't risk that, not even for Doc Emmett, who was quietly confident that he could eventually win an appeal, but he felt they wouldn't give his application serious consideration until he had served a full ten years of his sentence. He was still most of a year short of that.

Doyle decided to ride to Fort Smith, Arkansas. He might pick up a late trail herd there on its way to St Louis or one of the Kansas railheads before the end of the season. If he missed, then he would make for Indian Territory and head on down to the Red River country or Wichita Falls. Doyle knew that area pretty well – and the Territory, too, come to that. He and Jigger Bush with a few others had ranged back and forth all across there for years, raising hell.

But he didn't want to think about those outlaw years. He had plenty on his mind as it was.

As he rode, he kept fingering the watch in his shirt pocket. Somehow he reckoned this was the answer to something, but damned if he knew what: he had a hunch there was more than murder and a chancy theft to this deal. *Why had Doc taken the watch in the first place?*

It was only after he reached Fayetteville in northwest Arkansas that he realized he had a few nagging doubts about Emmett's story. Nothing he could put his finger on, but, like that judge and jury, he felt something wasn't quite right.

Fact was, he was uncomfortable about the whole damned thing and was beginning to wish he had never tracked down Tyrell.

Doyle sure hadn't figured to be back in St Louis so soon, but here he was, a few weeks after he had quit Big Robbie's outfit, penning cows down at the rail yards, swallowing the same old dust he had just gotten out of his system from last time.

This was a big Texas outfit run by the Comanche County Cattlemen's Association and they had been short a top-hand point rider when he had caught up with them camped on the White River flats outside of St Paul. The trail boss, a man named Amarillo Haines, had told Doyle he was welcome to feed at the supper fire, even spread his blankets with the crew for the night, but he had no jobs going, this close to the end of the trail.

By morning, he was short a point rider. The man had slipped away from his nighthawk duty, gone into St Paul and gotten himself killed in a gunfight. Amarillo shook his shaggy head, shoulder-length, string-coloured hair fanning about his leathery face.

'A good man, but weak where booze and women were concerned. Supportin' an invalid mother down in Pecos, Texas. Now I've got it to do, tellin' her she's short a son. He's got money comin' and I reckon the boys'll chip in. They're a good bunch. Help the old lady out some.'

'Wouldn't mind kicking in a dollar,' Doyle said and knew right off now he couldn't ask to replace the dead man: it might seem as if he was trying to buy favour by donating to the fund.

But Amarillo didn't take it that way.

'Right kind of you, mister. Don't s'pose you feel like ridin' point as far as St Louis for a couple weeks? Top-hand's pay, though don't reckon I can rightly cut you in on the trail bonus, it bein' such a short time. These boys've been ridin' for four months.'

'I'd be glad of the job, Mr Haines. Wouldn't want to cut in on the bonus deal you got going.'

'Pick a mount from the remuda and take position soon's you finish your coffee,' the trail boss said.

It was a quick drive – ten days, and that included one flooded river-crossing where they lost nine head and a horse drowned. The meathouse buyers were starting to pack up in St Louis, but a couple of shrewd ones hung around, hoping to pick up a last-minute bargain.

But they were no match for the horse-trading skills of old Amarillo Haines. He squared off the two bidders against each other by sharp manoeuvring and got a better price than either had initially offered. So Doyle got a small end-of-trail bonus anyway, and he hit the high-spots with the Comanche County crew.

The saloons were abuzz with talk about an attempted hold-up at the bank used by the meat-packers: naturally, its safe was full to overflowing with funds. Someone had given away the bandits' plan, and the lawman had deputized a bunch of townsfolk and they had laid an ambush. It was one hell of a shoot-out – five townsmen had died and seven more were wounded. But they got all five of the outlaws, shot them dead where they made their stand.

The bodies were lined up for display in cheap pine coffins outside the undertaker's. Idling past with a bunch of trail hands, Doyle casually glanced at the bullet-riddled bodies – and stopped in his tracks.

'What's up, kid?' asked the rugged wrangler. 'Never seen a dead man before?

Doyle swallowed, tried to smile. 'Not – shot to pieces like that.'

'C'mon. What you need is a shot of red-eye.'

Doyle allowed himself to be led on, even downed two shot-glasses of red-eye, before he felt that his heart was beating normally again.

One of those dead outlaws was Jigger Bush, half his face torn away by a shotgun blast. It shook the hell out of Matt Doyle: that was where he had been headed before Blood Creek. That year inside had done something for him, after all, he allowed, but sick in his stomach as he tried to forget the image of Jigger – *Live fast, die young* – Jigger's stated philosophy. *Well, Jigger, old pard: you made it but I don't envy you . . . .*

But he hitched at his gunbelt, determined to forget Jigger. No! Keep remembering him and the way he looked now. He'd stay on the straight and narrow if he did that . . . .

'Let's go tie a knot in the tail of the ol' curly wolf, boys!' he shouted suddenly and the Texans gladly took up the call, howling at the moon – or the barroom ceiling . . . .

Things got a mite out of hand and there were some crazy dares, one of which involved the faro and crap tables of the gambling section of Ace Kelly's saloon. Doyle, enjoying himself now, didn't realize these rough-tough Texans were pouring a slug or two of rotgut into every glass of beer he drank.

In no time at all his head was swimming and he was gambling recklessly, pushing money into the hands of the Texans, who kept reminding him that it was his turn to buy a round of drinks. It seemed to be 'his turn' constantly, but Doyle didn't notice, shook his head, trying to keep his vision clear, losing more than he was winning, egged on by the Texans who were enjoying their prank.

They meant no real harm; to these rough trail men money meant little. If their pockets were empty, why, hell, go work to fill 'em up again. What the hell was money for, anyway, if it wasn't for spending on a good time? Having fun, even at someone else's expense – literally.

But it all came to an abrupt end when the dealer boredly asked Doyle to cover his bet and the drunken young cowboy found he had no more money. The dealer started to turn nasty and signalled for one of the bouncers. Unfortunately, for Doyle, it was the same man who had thrown him down the stairs and beat-up on him a few weeks earlier. He saw Doyle and bared his teeth as he moved in.

Doyle, even through the fumes messing up his head, recognized the man, and didn't aim to feel those hammer-hard fists crunching his flesh again. He looked around but his newfound 'friends' were suddenly nowhere to be seen. Then, in a dazzling flash of drunken inspiration, he brought out the pocket-watch and held it so that the lamplight reflected from the case. It looked real enough in the yellow light. He pushed it across the table to the dealer.

'Worth twenty bucks . . . ?'

'Hell, it don't look like real gold!' The dealer placed it against one ear. 'Ain't even tickin'.'

'Come on!' growled the bouncer, reaching for the swaying Doyle.

'Wait! Ask Ace if he'll take it to cover the bet. Ask him!' Doyle was almost pleading.

After a hesitation, the dealer picked up the watch.

'Okay. I'll go ask.' He said in a lower voice to the bouncer. 'Them Texans've been spikin' his beer. Kid dunno where the hell he is or what he's doin'.'

'He'll know soon,' the bouncer said meaningfully.

'Just keep an eye on him till I get back.'

The bouncer shoved Doyle down into a chair and held him there while the dealer made his way through the tobacco smoke and crowds to Kelly's office.

The saloon owner didn't appear much interested in accepting the watch, able to tell from experience that it was just plated and not solid gold. He glanced at it cursorily, tossed it back to the dealer, but as the man turned to leave he suddenly said:

'Lemme have that again, Ford.'

Kelly really studied the watch this time, then opened the back, pursed his lips and said, 'Yeah, okay – let him cover his bet with this. But make sure he loses.'

That would be no problem, the dealer assured Kelly, and went back to the faro layout, placing the watch on the table.

'You're covered, kid. Now let's see you buck the tiger.' That was what they called a wild bet on faro, *bucking the tiger* . . . .

The dealer dealt his cards to Doyle who seemed to have trouble staying awake now. It took only a glance at the cards' total for him to realize he was now ragged-ass broke.

Nothing much seemed to register with him – he was too stunned – and then the grinning bouncer dragged him over to the side-door and stepped out into the night with him.

He awoke in a jail cell and for a terrified moment thought he was back in Blood Creek. But he had company. Most of the trail crew were crowded into the cell in various postures and levels of pain and remorse and sickness.

'Hangover House,' roared Amarillo Haines delight-edly as he stood out in the passage at the barred door, gaining pleasure from the way his booming voice made the sorry-looking bunch in the cell wince and cower. 'I've paid your fines. Now git out here and dunk your heads in the nearest hoss-trough. Then go down to the pens and start loadin' them cows on the train. Meathouse agent is waitin' and he ain't a patient man . . .'

Heads hanging, they began to shuffle past the trail boss, some murmuring 'thanks, boss', others just nodding, still others holding their heads in both hands. Amarillo reached out and stopped Doyle who was slack-faced and red-eyed and felt sick. One eye was swollen and his mouth was puffy.

'Not you, Matt. I heard the trick they played on you, spikin' your drinks, made you lose all your money. I'm givin' you ten bucks and a hoss. You can spend it any way you like. But you ever come to work for me again and it comes off the top of your wages. OK?'

'Obliged, Mr Haines. Much obliged.'

Doyle shook hands limply with the trail boss, then shuffled down the passage and out into the blinding sunlight which seemed to split his head open like an axe.

He squinted and reeled, jamming his hat on tightly, immediately regretting it because it made his headache worse. He needed a beer to get started for the day and then some six-shooter coffee . . . .

An iron grip numbed his arm and he staggered as he was hauled around roughly. His spirits sank way down when he recognized the bouncer from Kelly's saloon.

'What now . . .?'

The bouncer shook him and grinned sadistically as Doyle moaned.

'Mr Kelly wants to see you.'

'The hell for? He's got all I own!'

But by then the bouncer, a man named Grimm, as Matt later found out, and a mighty appropriate name it was, too, was dragging him down the street and into the saloon, upstairs to Kelly's suite, where Ace Kelly was sitting up in a double bed having breakfast off a tray. The auburn hair of a woman was spread out on a pillow beside him, one naked arm flung carelessly across Kelly's lap.

'You *look* as if you had a high ol' time last night, kid,' Kelly grinned. 'How much you remember?'

'Not much,' Doyle admitted.

'You recollect coverin' a faro bet with a gold watch, though, don't you?'

Doyle nodded. 'And losing it.'

Kelly reached under the pillow and held up the

52

watch on its twisted chain. Suddenly all the banter was gone and his eyes were hard, his voice cutting like a honed blade.

'Now, tell me just where you got this watch. And I'll warn you now, you lie to me and Grimm there'll tear your head clear off your shoulders and toss it into the latrine pit out back. So what's it gonna be, cowboy? Talk – or die?'

5
Tall Story

Cash Tyrell knew Amarillo Haines. They had trailed together years ago and had parted bad friends after a fist fight that began when Tyrell accused Haines of taking some money from his bedroll.

It turned out it was a man Haines had fired, and who had left Amarillo's clasp knife on the ground near the disarrayed bedroll so he would get the blame. Tyrell reluctantly told Amarillo he had made a mistake and Haines had said,

'You did and I don't aim to give you a chance to make another. Draw your time, Cash.'

So when Tyrell rode into the holding-pen area at St Louis, looking for Matt Doyle whom he had traced laboriously from Joplin, he swore when the man he had asked to point out whoever was in charge indicated the long-haired man keeping tally while sitting on the top rail of the corrals' entry chute.

But he rode on down and said quietly, still sitting in the saddle: 'Long time, Amarillo.'

Haines turned his head and his weathered face

showed nothing as he recognized Tyrell.

'Not long enough,' he said, turning back to his tally-book.

'Hell, you got a long memory. Admitted, I made a mistake, damnit.'

Haines glanced at the man again.

'But you never had the guts to say "sorry". You're a self-centred man, Cash, and I got no use for you.'

'OK, OK. All I want to know is did a feller named Matt Doyle get a job with you?'

Haines frowned. 'Why would you want to know who I hired or didn't?'

'Feller stampeded my herd down at the ranch, shot up one of my cowhands, beat me and robbed me. I been followin' his trail and I learned he calls himself Matt Doyle and someone said they thought he hired-on to the last herd comin' up-trail before end-of-season. Figured it might be you, but just hoped you wouldn't be along in person.'

'Always boss my own drives. This don't sound like Doyle to me . . . stealin', startin' stampedes.'

'So you did hire him. He still in town?'

'I've knowed you for a liar for a long time, Cash. Why should I believe you now? The feller I know as Matt Doyle is a decent young ranny, got prised loose from his bankroll last night in Kelly's saloon, even had to trade a pocket-watch to cover his faro bet.'

Tyrell grinned crookedly. 'He stole that watch from me!'

Anarillo frowned, called over a sweating cowhand to take the tallybook and clambered down stiffly. Something told him that Tyrell was speaking gospel now.

'Why would Matt Doyle rob you? He was with Big Robbie Macleay's bunch, but quit early after some fracas at Kelly's. Robbie said his men reckoned Matt was headin' for . . . By God! I b'lieve they said he was gon' to – Joplin.'

Tyrell's crooked grin widened. 'Yeah, my place. You know he done time in Blood Creek Pen?'

'Don't think he told me that. But didn't have to. I offered him the job after my point rider got himself killed.'

'Where is he, Amarillo? If he's in town. I'll find him, anyway, but you can save me a little time.'

The old trail boss shook his head. 'Dunno where he is. But someone said they saw him headin' for Kelly's saloon with that bouncer, Grimm . . .'

Amarillo wasn't sure but he thought Tyrell paled a little.

'Damn! Obliged, Amarillo, and I *am* sorry I thought you took my money that time.'

He wheeled and rode through the bustling, noisy railyards towards town, the fringe section that served the trail hands who brought in the big herds.

Amarillo scratched at his stubbled jaw: he hoped that boy would be all right . . . .

'Amarillo, I think I counted wrong!' called the man with the tallybook and Haines swore, turning back quickly.

Doyle figured he owed Cash Tyrell nothing and told Ace Kelly readily enough how he had taken the watch from the Joplin rancher.

But Kelly had shaken his head.

56

'Too easy, mister! We don't have enough – what you call it? Yeah: not enough – *motivation* here. But Grimm'll find out . . .' He pushed the auburn-haired woman out of bed and ignored her cries of complaint as she struggled to her feet, buck naked. 'Git!'

The men were silent as she dressed in front of them without embarrassment and when Kelly grew impatient, Grimm picked her up bodily, only half-dressed, and snapped at Doyle to open the door for him.

Matt did – and then jumped through, slamming it behind him.

He heard the cursing and the thud as the woman hit the floor and heard her scream. But by that time he was out the side-door and leaping down the outside stairway.

He didn't aim to stick around just to get beaten to a pulp by Grimm or anyone else.

The door above him wrenched open and Grimm roared. A man came around the corner at the end of the alley and Grimm yelled at him to stop Doyle. He was a townsman but a big one, and Doyle guessed he was used to obeying Grimm's orders when drinking in the saloon. The man lunged at Matt and he dodged under the thick arm that barred his way, slammed two lightning blows into the man's ribcage and sent him staggering. A heel caught on the edge of the boardwalk and the man went down, gasping.

Doyle leapt over him, glancing over his shoulder. Grimm came pounding out of the alley, just as the groggy townsman was struggling to his feet. Grimm cursed and tried to push him aside but the man clutched at him instinctively and both fell, rolling off the walk into the dust.

Doyle cut across the street through the early traffic, dodging horses and buckboards and one lumbering wagon, dived into a side-street and down an alley, his efforts blurring his vision, head shattering with each pounding step he took. He gave small involuntary moans as he ran, still not recovered from last night, wondering if he could make good his escape.

He found himself heading towards the railyards where there was a lot of activity with the loading of meathouse cattle, the loco steaming and panting, dust and din and men riding and running everywhere after cows that broke out of chutes or boxcars.

It was a good place to be, if a man was on the run.

With a little luck he could get lost in the confusion.

Then he figured his luck had run out, for as he rounded a bend he was almost trampled by a rider who hauled rein so hard the horse reared up on its hind legs. As the man gained control, and Doyle climbed to his feet, he saw the rider was Cash Tyrell.

Tyrell acted the faster, his sixgun coming up and covering Doyle, who was slowed down plenty by his hangover and exertions. Tyrell grinned.

'Well, now ain't this lucky! For me, that is!'

'Maybe not so lucky,' Doyle gasped, jerking a thumb over his shoulder. 'Grimm's somewhere behind me – sent by Kelly, because he wants to beat outta me the reason for giving you some grief – and stealing that watch!'

Cash Tyrell swore. 'Goddamn! I *knew* Ace'd buy in soon as Amarillo told me you'd put up the watch to cover your bet! You blamed idiot! Here! Climb up behind!'

Doyle needed no second bidding, figuring sticking with Tyrell was better than waiting for Grimm to catch up with him.

The rancher knew his way around the railyards, threaded through the maze of loading chutes and corrals and milling riders. He put the long cattle-train between them and the edge of town – and any pursuers paused by a line of the working cowhands' mounts tied to a hitch rail and shoved Doyle off.

'Grab a hoss and follow me! I can get you outta here with a whole hide if you show some sense.'

Doyle didn't argue and leapt onto a buckskin branded Cross H – Amarillo Haines's brand. Not that it mattered at this time, he figured, just so long as he got out of here before Grimm used him as a punching-and kicking-bag again.

But he still had to square up to Cash sooner or later.

Tyrell sure knew his way around East St Louis and after weaving through streets lined with drab red-brick ware-houses and small factories, he turned into a weed-grown street lined with dilapidated houses and shacks. Almost at the end, he stopped and led the way around a small lot with a sagging fence and a weathered clap-board cottage with a crooked porch standing in the midst of weeds and trash.

They stashed the horses out of sight in some clumps of brush under a small group of trees and went through a hole in the fence and up to the back door of the old house.

A woman answered Tyrell's knock after a long delay. She was tall, holding a gown about her, clutching it at the throat. She smelled of stale booze and cigarettes and blew upwards with a heavy underlip in an attempt to get some strands of string-coloured hair out of her reddened eyes. Her age was anyone's guess.

Tyrell greeted her with a lot more enthusiasm than she showed for him but she led the way into a small parlour that was surprisngly neat, though garish because of bright-red curtains and multicoloured cushions scattered about. Half-way into the room, she turned, hands on hips, the gown swinging open to show some bare flesh. She glared at Tyrell.

'Kinda late, ain't you, Cash? I heard about you a couple weeks back, whoopin' it up in Kelly's with that black-haired bitch they call The Claw! You din' bother lookin' me up then, did you?'

'Aw, Blanche, Kelly's an old friend, hadn't seen him in a coon's age. He gimme free board an' lodgin'. . . I couldn't pass that up.'

They argued and Doyle stood by, embarrassed some. He was edgy after the chase and suddenly cut in.

'Tyrell! What the hell're we doing here?'

Cash Tyrell blinked and seemed to realize they were wasting time. He nodded, turned to Blanche, took her shoulders between his hands. She struggled but not too hard.

'Blanche, honey, we need a place to stay for couple hours – till dark, say. We can pay.'

Blanche swivelled her gaze to Doyle who smiled, but the woman's face remained sober.

'On the run?'

'Just need a little privacy, Blanche. Got a deal to work out.' Tyrell smiled, took some money from his pocket and pressed it into the woman's hand. She snapped her head up when she saw the gold coin amongst the silver. 'Make up for my – missin' you last time, hon?'

She almost smiled, raised a hand as he reached for her again.

'I'll go out till dark. You be gone by the time I get back.'

'Sure, sure, hon, whatever you say, it's your place. Listen, you think you could make us somethin' to eat first . . . ?'

She snorted, starting out of the room.

'If you can find any grub in this dump you can eat it – if you're game!'

Twenty minutes later she left, wearing a feather-trimmed dress and a hat that slanted way over to one side of her head. She wore too much face-paint but her hair seemed to be arranged neatly. She didn't say farewell.

Tyrell blew out his cheeks, sat down on the edge of the sofa, looking at one of the garish satin cushions. *Granny's Doll House, Deadwood, Dakota*, was worked on it in yellow thread. Tyrell snorted.

'Wouldn't mind playin' with some of the dolls at Granny's. Was there once and —'

'The hell're we hanging around town for?' cut in Doyle, still edgy.

'Well, if it's true you put up that watch when you was buckin' the tiger in Kelly's, we gotta get it back.'

'The watch? No, sir, not me, I'm not going within a mile of that Grimm!'

Tyrell took out two cheroots, tossed one to Doyle who was pacing about, checking the windows frequently. When both smokes were going, the rancher said:

'Tell you a story about the watch – if you tell me what this "Emmett" told you.'

Doyle sat down in a worn chair. 'You're wondering if Doc Emmett told me something about that watch, aren't you?'

'Listen, his name ain't Emmett! He's Lang Dawson. Never uses his real name.'

Doyle recalled that 'Emmett' had told him in Blood Creek jail that anyone breaking the law who used his own name was a damn fool. Tyrell wanted to know everything that Emmett had told him but Doyle refused, then changed his mind when the argument looked like being protracted.

So he related the story Emmett had told him in jail, finishing with: 'He said you stole his money and the watch and caused him all the trouble he's now in.'

'Like hell! It never happened anythin' like that! He's just tryin' to make himself look good.'

'Well, what's your version?'

Tyrell was silent for a time then said, 'OK. Doc and me were pardners. We had some beeves for sale, not wearing their original brands. This Resnick was a meathouse buyer but on the side he dealt in rustled stock. Only he tried to gyp us this time and there was a fight and Resnick got killed. Me and Doc high-tailed it, after opening Resnick's safe with the key he had on him. We took his money and the watch was in there, too, and Doc grabbed that. Without goin' into details we busted up and I took the watch and the money and lit out. Heard a posse caught up with Doc and nailed him for Resnick's murder . . .' He shrugged. 'Luck of the game. You can savvy that if you've ever rode the owl-hoot.'

'You could've cleared Doc!'

There was cold accusation in Doyle's last words and Tyrell pursed his lips, shaking his head.

'Every man for himself, din' you ever learn that?'

'Not the way Doc figures. Anyway, I don't believe you. You come out smelling like roses too easy. Mr Goody.'

Tyrell's face was craggy, slit-eyed, *dangerous*. Doyle could well imagine him killing a man in cold blood for profit. Suddenly, Tyrell nodded as if to himself: he had reached a decision.

'OK, I can see you ain't a fool. Cut to the bone, it went like this: we tried to do a deal with Resnick. Not over rustled steers, though we'd sold him some at other times. No, we tried to do a deal on the watch.'

Doyle frowned. 'What the hell is it about that watch? It's only plated and it don't even work. The hands are frozen. I tried to move 'em but they won't budge.'

Tyrell nodded. 'Queer, ain't it? But it's important somehow. There was an old feller, name of Asa Larkin, up near St Jo. Had a place out on the Platte River and made a livin' supplyin' outlaws with grub and ammo and sometimes he'd hide 'em out if they had enough money. He took a shine to Dawson an' me after we pulled him outta the Platte one time when it flooded and a heap of big trees from upstream smashed through his shack and carried him down river. He'd been caught in the root system and the tree kept rollin' him under so he was near-drowned when we got him out. After that, we got supplies for nothin', could hole up there as long as we liked. He was beholden to us.'

'Where does the watch come in?' Doyle was on his feet, looking out the window again. 'D'you trust that whore, Blanche?'

Tyrell looked up sharply. 'Huh? Hell, no man but a damn fool trusts a whore. Don't worry, we'll be outta here in an hour – Kelly will've given up lookin' by then. Yeah, well, Asa often used to bring out this watch with some old stuff he'd collected, loved to talk about the "old days" as he knew 'em. Mighty interestin' life he led, buffalo-runner, whiskey- and gun-peddler, gold-miner . . .'

'Judas *priest*, Tyrell!'

'Huh? Oh, right. He said a man named Tom Resnick gave it to him.' He held up a hand quickly to stall Doyle's obvious question. '*Father* of the other Tommy Resnick.'

'Look, get to the point. I can jump ahead a bit and figure that you either stole the watch from Larkin or he left it to you because he was grateful you'd saved his life . . .'

'Yeah!' Tyrell said with some surprise. 'That's just what he done! Said the watch was real valuable and that he was gonna leave it to Dawson and me in his will.'

'He died then.'

Tyrell nodded jerkily. 'Tortured first. Put through hell, the poor old bastard. When we found him he was

64

chopped up somethin' awful – I lost my supper. He was barely alive but told us it was Resnick's son who'd done it to him, with a man named Usher who was Resnick's bodyguard. Said the watch was rightfully his and left Asa for dead . . .'

'So you and Emmett – or Dawson – went after Resnick to get the watch?'

'Resnick went crazy when he found out we even knew about it. He still had Usher with him, sicced-him on to us and that's what started the fight and a gun went off and killed Resnick. Usher had dived out a window by that time and just kept goin', but he stopped at a law office somewhere and gave 'em our names and a story how we'd killed Resnick in cold blood – and that's how Dawson ended up in Blood Creek jail.'

'While you stayed free – with the watch.'

Tyrell shrugged. 'Hell, weren't any sense in me buyin' in. I'd've been jailed, too. Funny thing, I had the watch valued and they told me it was junk. It didn't work, wasn't worth fixin', and was only lightly gold-plated. I just threw it into that metal box you stole from me and forgot about it.'

Doyle met and held Tyrell's hardening gaze and said: 'You wouldn't've kept that watch if you didn't figure it was still worth something – or *could* be worth something! All the other stuff in that box mattered to you: letters from your mother and sister, a lock of hair, likely your mother's, and that damn tooth!'

Tyrell was slightly flushed and uncomfortable.

'Belonged to my father – never knew him. Mother gave it to me. Dunno why she kept it . . .' He stopped, cleared his throat, standing now. 'No one calls me a liar, Doyle! Now take it back!'

'The hell I will! You've been spinning me tall tales. My head's swimming trying to figure which version to believe and I've had a bellyful! You *are* a damn liar!'

Tyrell swung a punch but Doyle rode it, blocked the second punch and ducked a third. Tyrell's knee caught his shoulder and sent him flailing over the chair. The rancher came at him, stomping, angry now. Doyle rolled in against the wall but a boot skidded across his forehead and that made him mad.

He hadn't wanted to hit Tyrell, because the man was so much older, but the rancher was mighty tough and had his dander up now. So Doyle kicked his legs from under him and bounded to his feet. As Tyrell started up, he kicked the rancher in the side. Tyrell staggered but rolled to his feet and hammered a barrage of blows at the younger man. Doyle covered and took most of them on his forearms, although two made his head ring. He weaved, brushed one of Tyrell's punches aside and hit him on the side of the square jaw. The rancher staggered back and Doyle went after him, forcing him against the wall, pummelling his thick midriff, feeling the man's legs sag. He slammed him in the belly, set himself for the finishing uppercut . . .

And then the door burst open behind him and he heard Blanche's bitter voice:

'*There*! Told you he'd be here! The two-timin' son of a bitch!'

Doyle stumbled as he turned quickly and then froze. Behind the scorned woman stood Ace Kelly and

66

Grimm, the latter holding a cocked sixgun in one of his large hands.

'Howdy, gents,' Kelly said affably. 'Good to see you again.'

6

'Don't Kill 'Em!'

Doyle and Tyrell were quickly disarmed and Grimm punched each man in the kidneys, dropping them to their knees.

Blanche gasped behind a hand she put to her mouth. No one took any notice. Kelly was concentrating on Doyle and Tyrell. He walked forward to stand behind them, fumbled in his pocket and thrust something in front of Tyrell's pain-contorted face.

'Tell me about it,' he snapped.

Tyrell focused on the watch and then looked up awkwardly at Kelly. 'Looks like a watch, Ace.'

Kelly sighed, nodded to Grimm. He twisted fingers in Tyrell's hair and slammed his head into the wall. The man moaned and writhed, sliding to the floor.

'Oh! Don't hurt him!'

Kelly glanced over his shoulder at the woman.

'You still here? Go take a walk or somethin'. You been paid.'

'I wouldn't've told you where they was if I'd known you was gonna hurt him!'

'Grimm! See her out!'

'I'm goin', I'm goin'!' Blanche said, quickly hurrying from the room as the bouncer glared balefully and took a step towards her.

Kelly kicked Tyrell where he lay on the floor.

'Cash, you stayed with me a week. We put away a heap of my bonded bourbon and we both ran off at the mouth some. You told me about this watch. I didn't recognize it when Doyle first sent it in to cover his faro bet, but somethin' jogged my memory. As I recollect, you told me this watch was mighty valuable. But you – didn't – tell – me – *why*!'

With each of his last words, Kelly kicked Tyrell in the side for emphasis. The rancher moaned, hurt, coughing, face twisted in agony. Doyle stayed put on his knees, his kidneys throbbing, awaiting his turn. He knew it had to come and he knew he was going to suffer plenty, because he had even less to tell Kelly than did Tyrell.

'Damn you, Ace!' Tyrell gritted. 'I *dunno* why it's valuable! I just kept it in the hope one day I might figure it out. But I hadn't looked at it in years. Then Doyle here stole it . . .'

Thanks heaps, Tyrell, you lousy son of a bitch! Doyle thought. *Just what I need is for you to draw attention to me!*

If it was a ploy by the rancher to take the heat off himself, it worked. Kelly and Grimm both turned to Doyle and Grimm cuffed him across the head, rammed a knee into his spine, crushing the front of his body against the wall. Doyle felt his nose start to bleed. Grimm kicked him in the spine.

'Seems to me you knew somethin' about this watch,'

drawled Kelly, at his ease. 'Otherwise you wouldn't've gone all the way to Joplin to steal it from Cash here . . .'

'I did it for Doc Emmett – my cell-mate at Blood Creek.' The words came hard and breathlessly and Doyle licked some blood from his upper lip. 'He asked me if I ever got a chance, to grab it, but I dunno what the hell it's all about.'

'Oh, is that so?' Kelly asked. 'Well, happens I don't agree with you. Grimm, I'm gonna leave you alone with these two for – aw, say half an hour. When I come back, I want 'em to tell me what I want to know, even if they have to mumble because you've kicked their teeth in. Savvy?'

Grimm's thick lips rippled into an ugly smile and there was a flare of anticipation in his hard eyes. He cuffed Doyle again.

'I won't need that much time.'

Kelly held up a hand, pausing in the act of lighting a cigarillo. 'No, you take it easy and do a good job, Grimm. I might pass the time with Blanche, she's old but she still knows how to pleasure a man . . .'

'I'll blow your damn pecker clear off your belly if you lay another hand on Cash!'

Startled, all four men looked quickly at the door where the voice came from. Blanche stood there, pale and nervous, eyes glistening with barely restrained tears, and holding a strange-looking long gun with over-and-under barrels. The top barrel was small-bore, like a rifle, but the underneath could not be mistaken for anything but what it was: a shotgun.

'Top barrel shoots a bullet,' Blanche said, her rough voice holding a slight tremor as her nervous hands moved agitatedly in their grip on the gun. 'Underneath's loaded with a 20-gauge shot shell. I've forgotten which way the lever goes on top so first one moves takes a chance whether he stops a bullet or a bellyful of buckshot!'

'Jesus, lady!' breathed Grimm holding out one hand in a cautioning gesture. 'Take it easy. Them old Savages can be mighty touchy!'

There were beads of sweat on Grimm's forehead. Kelly still seemed cool but there was a wariness about him now as he bored his gaze into the woman.

'Best if you don't do this, Blanche,' he said mildly. 'You know what I'll do to you afterwards.'

The gun wavered wildly as the words shook her. She licked her painted lips.

'Just shut up, Ace! You were always a mean bastard under that joky front you put on. You just do like I say or I swear I'll kill you first!'

Grimm nudged Kelly. 'She's like a hair trigger, boss! She'll blow us to hell if we mess with her.'

'You can believe that!' Blanche assured them, then swivelled her gaze to Tyrell and Doyle who were helping each other to their feet. 'You all right, Cash, honey?'

Tyrell nodded: he was a little leery of her, too.

Hell, there was no accounting for women! Ten minutes ago she betrayed him, now she was rescuing him! Well, the only thing he'd ever really understood about women was that they were built different to men – and that was something to be grateful for. Otherwise, he could never fathom them . . . .

He brought his dazed, wandering mind back to the present as Doyle slurred, holding a kerchief to his bleeding nose.

71

'Let's get the hell outta here, Tyrell!'

'Good idea,' Tyrell allowed. He stumbled a little as he went to the chair where Grimm had thrown their sixguns, picked up both weapons, selected his own and tossed the other to Doyle, who moved to stand in front of Grimm, stared hard and long into the man's eyes. They were small and cold with raw hatred.

'Never did like you, Grimm,' the cowboy said quietly, and gun-whipped the man to his knees with two brutal, slashing blows of his Colt's barrel.

Grimm grunted and swayed, a deep gash opening on one cheek, his hat on the floor, his eyes almost crossed. Doyle bared his teeth and brought up his knee savagely into the man's face. The bouncer went down without a sound, blood spread across his brutal features, splashing Doyle's trousers.

Tyrell nodded approval and stepped in front of Kelly.

'You're a sidewinder, Ace. My own fault. I forgot you're about the greediest bastard I've ever met, but I never figured you'd turn on me. We used to be pards – you, me, Dawson, Tommy Resnick, even old Larkin. We was a wild bunch but by hell we had us some *fun*, din' we? We raised hell across three states until we had that leetle fallin' out over the Wells Fargo Express depot in Dodge . . . But, that's water under the bridge long ago, ain't it?'

Kelly merely stared and Tyrell thrust his battered face close and shouted so loud that the saloon-man took a hurried step backwards. '*Ain't that so?*'

Kelly nodded and opened his mouth but didn't get a chance to speak. Tyrell brought up a knee into his crotch and as the man groaned and sagged sickly, clubbed Kelly to the floor, whipping the gun back and forth several times.

'*Now* we can get outta here!' Tyrell said, holstering his gun and turning to Blanche. He grinned, slid an arm about her somewhat ample waist, taking the rifle-shotgun from her with the other hand. He kissed her on the mouth. 'Thanks, Blanche – I won't forget this.'

She smiled, wiping some of his blood from her lips and punched him lightly in the belly.

'Next time you know where to come when you want a real woman. You forget all about that Claw bitch.'

Tyrell blinked owlishly. 'Who?'

Blanche smiled, pleased. 'Go on – get outta here.'

Tyrell picked up his hat and jerked his head at Doyle who frowned as he knelt beside the unconscious Kelly and took the watch from the man's pocket.

'What about Blanche? You can't leave her here to face Kelly and Grimm when they come round . . .'

Tyrell glanced towards the woman. 'You'll be all right, won't you?'

Her mouth stretched out a little before she nodded.

'I aim to be on the next train out – it leaves in twenty minutes.'

'What if you don't make it?' Doyle asked, genuinely concerned for her safety.

'Then I'll stay with a friend of mine until it's time for the Wichita stage, due to leave at nine tonight . . .'

'Come on, Doyle!' Tyrell growled impatiently. 'Whores're used to this kinda life – ain't nothin' to fuss yourself over.'

Blanche looked a little sad at this but Doyle thrust

73

out his right hand and, surprised, she took it.

'Thank you, ma'am – I surely appreciate what you done. If I get a chance I'll try to make it up to you some day . . . Good luck.'

'You, too, cowboy.' Blanche swivelled her gaze to Tyrell who was already heading for the front door. Doyle followed and she raised her voice a little. 'And, Matt – you shake Cash soon as you can! Keepin' company with him won't do you no good.'

Doyle paused as the rancher held the door open for him impatiently. Tyrell scowled.

'Just shut up, Blanche! Doyle – are you – comin'?'

Doyle nodded and said to the woman, a mite puzzled, 'I thought you were sweet on him?'

'Oh, I am,' Blanche replied. 'More fool me. Just can't help myself. But you take note of what I said, boy, or he'll get you killed.'

Grimm was the first to regain consciousness. His face was laid open to the bone and blood had flowed down his neck in a sticky flood.

It took him some minutes to recall what had happened and then he focused on Ace Kelly's moving form and helped the saloon-man to sit up against the wall. Kelly's face had changed. It looked lopsided, his nose hammered to windward, one eye was swollen almost closed and along his jaw was a bruised ridge. He rubbed gently at this place, working a bloody tongue around inside his mouth.

'You don't look too good, boss.'

'I look a helluva lot better'n Tyrell an' Doyle are gonna look when I catch up with 'em!'

Grimm stared at his bloody kerchief after taking it away from the deepest gash in his face.

'Still bleedin'. I'll need a couple stitches, then I'll get some of the boys and we'll light out after the bastards! I'll bring you Doyle's head.'

'*No!*' snapped the saloon-man angrily, his one visible eye glinting with – something – something *bad*. 'No, don't kill 'em. I want 'em both alive. They'll die when I say they die and that won't be for a long, painful time.' He spat some blood. 'Besides, I think that kid might know more about the watch than he was tellin'. He spent a year in Blood Creek with Dawson. He must've picked up somethin' or he wouldn't've gone after Tyrell.'

Grimm nodded, easing slowly to his feet, grimacing.

'What about Blanche?'

Kelly lifted a hand and let it flop back into his lap. 'If she's still around, do what you like with her. If she's gone, forget about her – we got more important things than worryin' about some old whore.'

Grimm looked disapppointed, helped Kelly into a chair and then went out, weaving, still holding a kerchief against his face.

Kelly sat there, breathing hard, thinking about just what he would do to Doyle and Tyrell when he caught them.

Tyrell led the way out of St Louis. Doyle became lost after the first few minutes as they raced their mounts through twisting alleys, down dead-end streets that Tyrell somehow found a way out of, across weed-grown lots, through a large brick warehouse of some kind, dodging workmen and stacks of crates and even two unassembled wagons. With curses from the men ringing in their ears, Tyrell led the way into a whole industrial area that took them fifteen minutes to clear and then they were well into the western part of St Louis where it spilled over into the State of Missouri.

'You know where you're going?' Doyle called, his head spinning with all the sudden changes of direction.

'Just keep followin'. Kelly's gonna send men after us but I'm hopin' he'll waste some time lookin' around the railyards, figuring as we're both cowmen we might try to ride out on the meathouse trains. Only thing is, good ol' Ace has a helluva lot of men he can call on. Might be able to split 'em up and check out several directions at once.'

Doyle nodded resignedly. 'Let's light a shuck then – and I mean in a hurry!'

'We'll be okay. You wanna gimme that watch in case you lose it?'

Doyle merely laughed.

They almost made it clear without being seen.

Just as they started along the trail to Clayton, figuring to cut out after a mile or two and swing south, they heard the first shot. Just before it, Doyle had caught the buzz of something to his left, thinking it was an insect for they had seen wild bees hovering about the flowering branches of bushes. Now, ahead, he saw the puff of dust and knew it was the first bullet.

Tyrell saw it, too, and behind, a group of four horsemen closed in, riding hard, one man with the reins between his teeth as he threw his rifle up to his shoulder. There was a greyish line of gunsmoke, quickly dispersed by the wind, and once again the fugitives heard the dull buzz of hot lead cutting through the air.

Doyle started to unlimber his rifle from the saddle scabbard.

'Quit that!' Tyrell yelled. 'They ain't gonna hit us shootin' like that – we're at extreme range. Let 'em waste lead. Use your spurs, there's a creek around that next bend. Shallow, as I recall. We get across, we can rig an ambush.'

Doyle pushed the Winchester back into the scabbard and spurred after the rancher. He didn't care for water-crossings when a posse was after him. He had seen too many men caught half-way by the pursuers, easy targets, their blood turning the water red . . . .

But if Kelly's men weren't likely to hit them right now, Doyle knew he and Tyrell stood just as little chance of hitting them. So, the wisest thing was to ride hell for leather and get across that creek.

He didn't know how long it was since Tyrell had seen the creek but it was no longer a shallow crossing. Deep, green-brown water flowed between high banks and they would have to fight their mounts upstream to find a place that would allow them to ride out with some sort of ease.

But Cash Tyrell didn't waste time on cursing; he raked his spurs and jumped his whinnying mount off the bank into the water. Doyle hesitated, but knew now he had no choice: any moment Kelly's men would come racing in on them.

With a bad feeling, Doyle and his mount plunged

into the water and he felt the current snatch at the horse right away. He had to force its head around to angle across the current, upstream, towards the only possible place for exit. He was holding his rifle now and had to control the horse with his knees and one hand on the reins. The animal wanted to go with the flow, of course, using its instinct, but Doyle stubbornly followed Tyrell although he felt letting the current carry them might yet be the best move: it flowed at a good, fast rate.

He saw Tyrell was having the same trouble with his mount and then the animal eventually managed to get itself turned downstream and the swearing rancher drifted down on him. Doyle deliberately wrenched his own mount's head around. Together they were hurled downstream by the current and even as Tyrell yelled there was no way up the banks down there, Kelly's men rounded the bend and came in a'shooting.

Bullets ripped and tore the water. Tyrell's mount whinnied and seemed to lurch. The current hurled them towards the far bank, suddenly changed and pushed them back towards the one where the killers were shooting.

'They're aimin' for the hosses!' Tyrell yelled.

'Quit leather then!' Doyle called back and kicked free of the stirrups.

'Are you loco?' Tyrell ducked as lead ricocheted from his saddle horn.

Doyle was already in the water, letting his mount swim free, knowing its instincts would give it the best chance. The current tumbled and rolled him and he tried to hold his rifle above the surge but not with complete success.

Then Tyrell saw why Doyle had left his mount.

There was a big tree caught slantwise to the current. Doyle snatched at a root, his arm almost wrenched out of its socket, boots scrabbling for a hold on the slimy wood.

He wedged himself in against the trunk, hooking one elbow over another root.

Tyrell's body came hurtling toward him and he reached out, thrusting his rifle at the man as he rolled and gagged. Tyrell grabbed hold and Doyle pulled him in, the current trying hard to snatch the man from his grip, bullets now chewing splinters off the log as the riders thundered along the bank, figuring they had easy targets,

But *they* were the easy targets.

Doyle and Tyrell had a tolerably firm and steady position to shoot from: the log rolled a little this way and that with the force of the current, but it was stable enough for them to aim straight.

When the first horse went down on shore, the others piled into and over it. A second rider was thrown and the other two had to concentrate on fighting their mounts to stay in the saddle. Tyrell shot one man and the bullet slammed him clear over the horse's rump with its impact. The second man stood in stirrups and fired a wild volley. Doyle's shot doubled him over and he dropped his rifle, one arm dangling. He got his horse turned and rode back into the trees.

The two men who had fallen off their horses fired several shots, but one broke, running after his mount.

Tyrell led him and nailed the man just as his hand closed on the trailing reins: he went down in a dusty tumble. The other man had had enough, he threw his gun away and, arms and legs pumping, made a break for the trees, hurried along by Doyle's singing lead.

'Kill the son of a bitch!' yelled Tyrell, reloading.

'Don't need to – he's out of it now.'

Tyrell glared. 'Yeah – I guess. Now all *we* gotta do is get out, too.'

'Shouldn't be a problem,' Doyle said, clinging to a root and indicating the far bank.

Both dripping horses stood there, shaking themselves, snorting and whinnying: probably they had enjoyed their swim – and, obviously, they had found a place to escape the river.

With rifles rammed into the backs of their belts, the two men struck out away from the tree trunk, the current reaching for them, spinning them, flinging them first right, then left and eventually into a shallow whirlpool. Here they floundered and clambered up a three-foot bank – Tyrell fell back twice, but he made it on his third raging attempt. They sat down, panting, rifles upended to drain any creek water from the barrels. The horses trotted across, nudging them.

'Let's get the hell outta here,' Tyrell said. 'I know a place we can hole up.'

'Good. There's a few questions I'd like to ask you.'

One foot in the stirrup, Tyrell glanced around at Doyle, frowning, eyes wary.

'Yeah? What?'

'Well, for one – I find it mighty interesting you said you used to be pards with Kelly – and Resnick and

Dawson, even Larkin. I think you been fibbing to me about that watch, Cash, old *amigo*.'

7
Hideout

Tyrell's hideout was across the wide Missouri.

It took them two days to get there, riding zigzag trails, cutting through canyons that narrowed so abruptly, that they had to dismount and lead their weary horses. There were steep drops and near-vertical climbs in a type of country Matt Doyle had never seen before.

They were exhausted by sundown and turned in after a silent supper. They skipped breakfast, opted for eating jerky or cold rabbit in the saddle.

And all the time they watched each other warily.

Doyle hung the watch around his neck on a leather thong, buttoned his shirt collar tight before turning in. Then they came to the big river and he wondered about Tyrell's sanity at even contemplating a crossing of this width of water. Hell, a man couldn't even see the far bank in this section, or just a hazy line of colour. It must be at least a mile across. But Tyrell knew his rivers and they crossed easily enough, only briefly swimming the horses in the very middle where the channel was deepest.

The rancher led the way through cutaways choked with brush to a kind of open cave. It was really a deep gouge beneath a huge overhang of rock and there were signs where many camp-fires had burned here over the years.

'They say Bloody Bill Anderson and his men used this place and a lot of other Civil War raiders, too. Old Asa showed it to me and I've used it several times. Helluva place when the rain comes from the nor'east, though. Blows right in.'

Doyle glanced up at the silver-blue stars scattered on a cobalt carpet, the moon still low down, touching a broken-saw range with a ghostly light.

'Sure is a pretty night,' Doyle opined. 'Used to get a glimpse of the stars through the cell window and I swear some nights I wanted out so bad I got the notion I could squirm between the bars and fly right up there.'

When he looked down again at the new fire, Tyrell was covering him with his sixgun.

'Reckon I better take care of that watch now, Matt.'

Doyle was close to the fire, sighed and reached up behind his neck to untie the leather thong.

Tyrell smiled. 'Now you're showin' some sense, boy . . .'

Then the gun went off as he reared backwards, wildly fending off the blazing brands from the newly lit fire that Doyle kicked into his face. Doyle stepped across the remains of the fire, planted a boot on

Tyrell's gunhand, using his weight, twisting until the grimacing rancher released his hold on the Colt. Doyle kicked it out of reach and while Tyrell sat up again, retrieved the gun and rammed it into his belt. The rancher sat there, glowering, rubbing his wrist.

'You can be downright mean when you want, boy!'

'You better believe it.' Doyle sat down on a rock, gesturing with his own gun. 'Might's well get the fire going and cook that turkey we shot this afternoon.'

Tyrell muttered as he began to pluck the feathers from the dead bird. Doyle watched for a time until it had been gutted and set on a stick in two forked supports above the licking flames.

'Better tell me about this damn watch, Tyrell. I'm getting mighty tired of hearing lies. I can figure you were all in a gang – you, Dawson, Resnick, Larkin and Ace Kelly. You robbed the Wells Fargo Express office in Dodge – and I think I recall hearing about that. Lot of money involved. Guess that's what your falling-out was over . . .? The shares?'

Tyrell's wrist was swollen, the skin torn, and he rubbed some neatsfoot oil into it, not looking up at the other.

'What I told you about me and Lang Dawson rescuin' Larkin was true. He'd worked for Wells Fargo for years and they caught him doin' some kinda deal: sellin' time tables of stages carryin' express boxes with a lot of loot and so on. They fired him and he was mighty riled. By way of showin' his appreciation for me and Dawson savin' his neck in the flood, he put a deal to us: he'd tell us where they hid the key to the big safe in the Dodge City Express office and we could grab ourselves a heap of *dinero*. He wanted one-third and the rest could be split any way we wanted between us and any other members of our gang.'

'Fair enough, I'd say.'

Tyrell snorted. 'You're still wet behind the ears where ridin' the owl-hoot's concerned, Matt! Anyways, it went off okay, but there was a deal of shootin'. I was hit, so was Ace. Posses were everywhere and we had to ride clear across two states before we shook 'em. Yeah, you're right. Everyone wanted a bigger share than they'd agreed on – except Asa. He only wanted one iron-bound express box, not much larger than a cookie tin. He wouldn't tell us what was in it, but he took it, ran off our hosses and rode out, leavin' us to sort out our troubles.

'Which we did, sort of, no one really happy, but we split and went our separate ways. Kelly gambled his and built on it so's he could open his saloon; Resnick bought into a cattle agency, took over, started buyin' for the meat houses —'

'Running rustled beef on the side?'

'Hell, it was a natural. He'd've been a fool to pass up the chance. I set myself up on a small spread; I'd been hit bad in that Dodge City deal and nearly died and it scared me some. Decided to go straight for a while.'

'What went wrong?' Doyle asked shrewdly.

Tyrell grinned. 'Well, when I was feelin' better – you know. Wideloopin' didn't seem like much. Anyway, Dawson went his own way, said he had a family he was gonna take care of. None of us knew about it before but that's what he claimed. 'Course, he might've given 'em some money from his share, but wasn't long before he was ridin' owl-hoot again, talked me into a few deals. Then one day we rode into Larkin's to arrange to push some runnin'-ironed beef through the system and found him all chopped up. And, like I told you, he said Resnick done it and Tommy took his watch . . . That's what he kept talkin' about, his damn old watch, but he din' have much spark left in him and he died without sayin' why it was worth so much.'

'But you took it off Dawson . . .'

Tyrell shrugged. 'Me and him were on the verge of bustin' up again, anyway. I tried everythin' with that watch, took it apart, even, but there's nothin' there – no map or instructions, not a goddamn thing. Couldn't even move the hands. But I couldn't bring myself to throw it out. Asa was dyin' in a welter of blood but all he could think of was that watch. It *has* to be worth somethin', or can point the way to somethin' that's worth heaps.'

'Like that iron-bound express box Larkin took?'

Tyrell's eyes narrowed. 'You ain't dumb, are you? Yeah, there's somethin' in that box. And he hid it away good. I've been back to Asa's old place several times, dug up all round. Nary a sign of the box . . .'

Doyle rolled a cigarette and tossed the makings to the rancher. He lit up.

'Dawson – or 'Doc' as we knew him in Blood Creek – got that nickname because he was always reading books in the library. The warden even bought in some he asked for, thinking he was trying to improve himself. The men reckoned he wanted to be a professor and they called him 'Prof' at first but it got whittled down to 'Doc'. I reckon he found out something. He made a lot of notes, studied a lot of maps, never let me near 'em. He had a box under his bunk he used to lock 'em in.'

Tyrell scowled, lit his cigarette from a burning twig from the fire, turned the turkey around on its spit.

'He always was a reader, Dawson. Used to study newspapers. Fact, we did several jobs he found out about from newspapers: when banks got big cash deliveries, trains with full safes in their express cars. Yeah, could've found out somethin'. He asked you to steal that watch from me?'

'Not just like that. He saved me from a real bad time in the pen and a couple of other times stood by me. I owed him plenty. When I was being released he said to me: "Remember the name Cash Tyrell. You ever hear it, track down the *hombre* who uses it. Rob him blind, bust him down good, the son of a bitch, but most of all, see if he's still got a gold watch." And he described it.

'I wanted to do something to repay him for taking care of me in jail so I swore I'd do it. He said to take or send the watch to his daughter, Claire. That he'd get it eventually, when his appeal was granted.'

Tyrell stiffened. 'So Claire's his kin! He talked about her but I thought she was some sorta girlfriend. We weren't all that close, just used to meet for jobs. Don't s'pose you recollect where she might be?'

Doyle frowned, then nodded slowly. 'He told me the town, was all.'

The rancher smiled and there was a lot of relief in it. 'Matt, *amigo*, you can have *both* drumsticks of that there turkey! Or any other sweetmeat you want. Long as you take me to this Claire! We got a deal?'

87

Doyle knew now that if ever he was going to find out what that goddamn watch meant, this was the time to do it. Tyrell had figured something out as soon as Doyle told him about Dawson's daughter . . . .

'Yeah, OK, Cash. But, you just follow on. I ain't about to *tell* you where she is. You want to find out, you tag along . . . and do what you're told.'

'Pleasure, Matt, me boy, pure, twenty-four-carat pleasure!'

And Tyrell roared with laughter.

The sound made Doyle more leery than ever.

Okay, that was it! 'Doc' Dawson (known as Dan 'Doc' Emmett in Blood Creek penitentiary) decided. *They threw out my Appeal and won't let me apply for parole for another five years. Well, I ain't about to wait, Your Lousy Honour, I ain't about to wait at all . . .!*

His mind was made up now: he had exhausted all avenues of the appeal procedure to get his sentence reduced and by sheer bad luck, the judge was a dyspeptic sour-gut named Halloran who wouldn't even give him time to spell out all his arguments or their legal basis. Doc saw right off he didn't stand a chance.

So, he was through trying the legal way to get out of here – which only left the other way. *Il*legal and he meant as illegal as a man could get.

Break-out.

Easier said than done, but ol' Doc hadn't just been reading about the law all these years. He had managed to locate a book on American penitentiaries and found, in the illustrated section, rough general plans of prisons, nothing too specific, but showing the broad layout and the drainage systems and a section dealing with foundations.

At the time he had thought – facetiously, because he was confident he could get out through loopholes in the legal system – that a man could probably plan an escape, using these sketches. Each jail was built to a basic concept: governments were always trying to save money and by using a tried-and-proven design could more accurately budget for the construction of prisons when and where necessary. A man might even escape on his first attempt, if he figured things carefully. And Dawson sure aimed to do *that*.

He hadn't thought about it in a long while, still preferring to earn a pardon and truly be a free man.

Now he would have to set to work and devise a way out of here. He already had some ideas. The drains were a distinct possibilty, as was a small tunnel under the foundations on the west wall which was 'balanced' on the pinnacle of a massive underground rock. Some engineer, puffed up with his own importance, had submitted the illustration, showing how striking bedrock did not necessarily mean abandoning construction and finding another location for the wall. His idea had been to bridge the hollows either side of the pinnacle with steel girders, which could take the weight of the wall, to the next section of solid ground. Of course, there were restrictions on the length of the girders, but a full page of calculations showed how the problem could be beaten by using squat, oversized iron-reinforced concrete pillars to support the girders' span.

The first prison to have such a wall was the one at

89

Blood Creek . . . and it was a success. Which probably explained how come the engineer had such an overblown notion of himself and why his illustration appeared in the book.

But the man had overlooked one thing: where the girders were laid, there was a gap beneath – they were supported at intervals by the massive iron and concrete pillars sure enough, but there was enough room *between* these pillars for a man to squeeze through easily.

Of course he would have to dig a tunnel to get that far first, but once under the wall he had only a little more dirt to move, angling upwards, and soon he would surface – *outside the prison*!

Dawson smiled as he lay on his bunk in the dark, hands locked behind his head, thinking about it, seeing that illustration as plainly as if he was looking at it in the book. He already knew he could reach that girder-supported wall foundation from one of the drainage tunnels. A distance of only twenty-five feet. Soft soil all the way . . .

Hell, he could be out of here in a few days.

He had been here long enough to know ways and means of spending time in the drains, with the right tools. It would be easier with a partner, though.

Doc Dawson unlocked his fingers and poked at the mattress a couple of feet above him where a recent prisoner named Mort Thoms was snoring. He was doing two years for rustling and was already showing signs of desperation after only a couple of months. He was old and rheumatic.

'Hey, Mort,' Dawson called quietly through the

darkness. 'Wake up! Din' you tell me once you worked in the mines down in Mexico, shoring-up tunnels . . .?'

'Wha – ? Hell, that was a long time ago. Kinda liked the work but too blamed hard. Couldn't do it now.'

'How's your memory?' Dawson asked.

8
Claire

Cash Tyrell had to hand it to Matt Doyle – the kid had a head on his shoulders and he knew how to use it.

Who in Hades would expect them to go south by riverboat!

But that's what they were doing. The young cowboy didn't give any kind of a hint where Claire Emmett-Dawson might be, but he knew more about the State of Missouri than Tyrell had figured.

After lying low in the riverbank hideout for a couple more days to make sure Kelly's men weren't in this neck of the woods, Doyle said,

'Okay – we ride for St Charles.'

Tyrell blinked. 'The hell for?'

'Catch the riverboat..Hooks up with the Mississippi north of St Louis and we go right on through under Kelly's nose.'

'By God! That's chancin' it, boy!'

'Why would Kelly think we'd be loco enough to make our way back through St Louis? Just plain logic would tell anyone we'd be staying as far away from there as we could. He won't be watching the riverboats.

Unless he has a gambling concession on them . . .?'

'Don't think so – no, I'm sure of it. That week I stayed with him he said he'd like the concession but the price was too high. Just might work, Matt, me boy! Just might work . . .'

'One thing – you good for the fares?'

Tyrell pursed his lips, glared, then nodded curtly.

'OK – I'll pay. But this better not be no wild-goose chase!'

It was only a few hours' ride to St Charles and they found a weathered and dog-eared riverboat schedule nailed to a trailside tree just outside of town. There was one sailing just on dark and that suited them fine.

They lay low, were lucky enough to find a bunch of cowpokes who were going aboard with their horses and joined them, taking their own mounts. The boat sailed on schedule to the usual town brass band blaring out *Watch Over My Rover*, and they stayed below decks until the lights of St Charles dropped behind.

It was a boring, five-day journey and they were continually alert each time the steamer pulled into the river towns and new passengers trooped on board. There were plenty of stops and Tyrell was growing restless the further south they steamed.

'Man, we'll be down far as Tennessee soon!' the rancher complained. 'We crossed the Illinois line yesterday!'

'Not much longer,' Doyle assured him.

They had stopped at Herculaneum, Crystal City, St Genevieve and Chester and then there was a long run through dangerous shallows where the boat twisted and turned, caught up once, and all the males had to go overside in thigh-deep water and put their shoulders to long poles before the thrashing stern-wheel pushed them clear. They rounded Cape Girardou, picked up a party from a rowboat midstream in the dead of night off Cairo, and then made a fast run down to New Madrid.

Here, Doyle suddenly said over breakfast, 'Better go saddle up after we've eaten.'

Tyrell snapped his head up. 'We're leavin'? Well, thank Christ for that! I was workin' out a plan how I could push you over the side and still get that damn watch off your neck before you took it under with you.'

Doyle grinned. 'Dunno whether to believe you or not, Cash, but there's a good chance you're speakin' gospel.'

Tyrell grunted and shovelled food hurriedly into his mouth. 'Let's get movin'!'

They left the steamboat at New Madrid, caught the big rope-drawn ferry across to the Tennessee side of the river, then Doyle led the way south for a day and they crossed the Big Muddy once more south of Steele at a place called Halfway Point.

'Halfway to where?' grumbled Tyrell. 'Hell?'

'Mebbe. We're nearing the home stretch now, Cash. And in case you haven't noticed, we're now in Arkansas.'

'Judas, I'm doin' more travelling this week than I did in a goddamn month ridin' owl-hoot!'

'Couple more days and we'll be there.'

Tyrell was silent and surly during the ride. He didn't know this country and had no idea where Doyle was taking him. That was what galled him – he couldn't even make a guess because he wasn't familiar with the names of towns in this neck of the woods.

They came to a place called Pocahontas on the Black River's eastern fork, and topped up their supplies, including a shared box of cartridges for the rifles and pistols. That was when Tyrell knew they were getting close. And once again Doyle was using his know-how, making sure they had grub and ammo before they reached their destination.

Just because they were looking for a girl, didn't mean she mightn't have male back-up waiting to argue with them.

'Wouldn't've minded ridin' the owl-hoot with you, boy. You show a lot of promise.'

Doyle was sober as he said, 'Only promise I made myself when I got out of Blood Creek was to go straight as I could. I didn't like my first taste of jail and I never want to go back.'

'Never been in one of the big pens,' mused Tyrell. 'Done a little time on a local chaingang down in Texas once and a month in Fort Smith's hoosegow for sassin' the Hangin' Judge. Son of a bitch kept me wonderin' every day of that month whether he was gonna string me up or not. Rode me outta town on a rail and told me never to come back.'

Doyle raised his eyebrows. 'And here we are in good old Arkansas.'

'Just don't expect me to go nowhere near Fort Smith, is all . . . Now, you gonna tell me where we're headed?'

Doyle pointed slightly west of north. 'Thataway.'

'Aaaaagh!' Tyrell spat in frustration but settled down

and by sundown they were riding into the mean-looking streets of a place called Calico Creek and Doyle announced: 'This is the place where Doc said his daughter is living.'

'You know just where?'

'No – but ought to be easy enough to find. Can't be too many Claire Emmetts or Claire Dawsons in a place this size.'

But by the time they were ready to turn in after ten that night no one in town whom they had asked could help them. They were a wary kind of folk and it was obviously a dirt-poor town. Some didn't even bother to answer. Others shook their heads before they had finished asking their question, and those who did answer were curt and emphatic.

'No one of that name in this town, mister.'

And then they moved on . . . .

Doyle thumbed back his hat, pushed a shoulder against a paint-peeling post supporting a sagging awning on a corner near a barber shop with a nailed-up door and took out the makings.

' "Easy to find her", huh?' gritted Tyrell, scrubbing a hand around his stubbled jaw. 'Guess you never thought to ask Dawson if she was married?'

'No, never did, Cash,' admitted Doyle. 'He just said his daughter Claire lived in Calico Creek and I took it for granted her name would be Emmett – till I met you and then figured maybe she was using her real name of Dawson. Never thought about her being married with some other name.'

'You ain't so damn smart then!'

'Well, we're here aren't we?'

Tyrell looked about the ill-lit town and spat when a gust of dry, dust-laden wind flapped his vest about his lean middle.

'*Jesus Christ*!' he said with feeling.

Grimm wasn't eager to see Ace Kelly but figured it had to be done and now was as good a time as any.

He was filthy from nigh on a week in the saddle, clothes stinking and rotting on his body, only dried sweat and crusted dirt holding them together, he reckoned. The others in his crew weren't any better and a couple were even worse off for he had had to beat up on them when they started bitching so much he could see a mutiny in the ranks coming.

He sent them to the bath-house and told them to have a night on the town and charge it to Kelly – something else he would have to explain at some time.

But right now he knocked briefly on the door of Kelly's office and came in, moving with saddle-stiffness as he closed the door behind him.

'Holy Hell! what's that stink?' cried Kelly, jerking his head up from the accounts he was working on at his desk. 'Judas, you look like you been caught in a buffalo stampede and all of 'em had diarrhoea! Goin' by the smell!'

'It's been rough, Ace.'

'Aw, poor ol' Grimm have a hard time, did he? Ridin' trail and doin' the job I pay him for and now he wants a pat on the head. How about you lie down on your back with all four paws in the air and I'll scratch your belly?'

'Yeah, all right, all right,' growled Grimm irritably,

97

making for a leather chair.

'Don't you sit down!' Kelly roared, half standing. 'You stay away from my furniture – *Don't touch nothin!* Just say what you have to and go get cleaned up. *Plllllease, get cleaned up!'*

Grimm sighed. 'It's been more'n a week and there's nary a sign of 'em, boss,' Grimm told him, deciding to make this formal and short now; it was plain there was no sympathy here for him and the hardships he had endured.

'No sign of 'em!' echoed the saloon-man, his face still not yet healed. He was glad to see the gash on Grimm's cheek was red and infected. 'What the hell'd they do? Sprout wings and fly away?'

'Might as well have for all the sign we picked up.'

'Then you weren't tryin' hard enough!'

Grimm had had enough. He sighed, holding himself in but right on the edge now.

'Boss, we busted our backs lookin'. They killed two of the boys at Wicks' Creek, wounded another. We hardly found a track after that and if you think we were slackin' . . .'

Grimm paused at the savage look Kelly threw his way: maybe this wasn't yet the time to speak rough . . .

'Boss, we really looked high and low, spread some dough around. Someone said they seen 'em headin' towards the Missouri River and we rode clear up there – we been to St Charles even —'

'St Charles!'

'Well, we was desperate and we figured they just might've jumped a riverboat. Got a man checkin' it out properly 'cause there was a bunch of cowpokes went

98

aboard with their mounts . . .'

Kelly scowled. 'You really think they'd be loco enough to ride a riverboat back through St Louis?'

'Like I said, we was desperate . . .'

'Aw, go get cleaned up and have a sleep. We'll talk about this in the mornin'. And by God you'd better come up with somethin' better than "we really tried, boss"! Savvy?'

Grimm nodded resignedly and shuffled his way out.

Ace Kelly thrust the account books away; no use trying to concentrate on them now. Instead, he rang for the woman with the auburn hair.

She would help pass the time more pleasantly.

The town didn't seem any friendlier in the light of the new day. In fact, it was overcast and this only emphasized the town's drabness. Folk moved about the street with a gait that made a man think they were doing it only because they had to, not because they had any enthusiasm for whatever reason they had ventured out of doors.

The general store was well stocked and well patronized but the crowds mostly looked blankly at Doyle when he asked his question about Claire. The storekeeper said gruffly, 'No one called Dawson or Emmett in this town, mister, and I oughta know, seein' as I've got the Post Office concession, too. B'lieve you were told that last night.' He gestured lazily to a wired-off cubicle with pigeon-holes.

'Could be I've got the name wrong,' Doyle admitted. 'Anyone at all you know lives here named Claire? That might be enough . . . ?'

99

No answer, so he bought some tobacco and vestas and left. On the boardwalk outside, he rolled a smoke with the fresh tobacco and crisp new papers and heard the store's door open behind him. A middle-aged woman with a worn look came struggling through with an armload of purchases and he fired up, stepped across to help her load them into a battered buckboard parked at the kerb.

'Thank you, young man.'

He smiled and touched a hand to his hatbrim, helped her up into the driving seat. She picked up the reins, ready to slap them across the rumps of the two patient horses, then looked directly at Doyle as he stepped back on the walk.

'Out of town, couple miles south, a farm there, just a widow-woman takin' care of it and not makin' much of a job of it, tho' she do seem to try hard enough.'

'Yes, ma'am?'

'Don't have much to do with the town. Likes to be what she calls self-sufficient. No one knows her name for sure – she don't get mail and don't send none. Be about twenty-five.'

He touched his hatbrim again. 'Thank you, ma'am.'

'One good turn deserves another,' she said crisply, lifted the reins and set the buckboard rolling with a couple of hoarse curses that widened Doyle's eyes.

He grinned to himself, shook his head, and went in search of Tyrell who was working the other side of the dusty street.

When they collected their weary mounts, the livery man seemed to brighten up.

'Leavin' us, huh? Guess you can see there ain't

much here for you – nor anyone else come to that.'

'We might be back,' Tyrell told him, just to see the man's face straighten out.

Then he frowned deeply. 'Why'd you want to do that?'

'Me and my pardner kinda like the look of the place. Thinkin' of startin' up a livery stables.'

'Hey! You can't do that! *I* got the livery here! Ain't room for *two* stables in this dump.'

'Well, mebbe one can move out.' Tyrell looked at Doyle soberly. 'That can be arranged, cain't it, Matt?'

Going along with the ribbing, Doyle dropped a hand to gun butt and nodded solemnly, narrowing his eyes, hoping he looked mean.

'Pleasure to do it.'

'Yeah. Just like that feller in Black Rock – only he didn't move far, just a little ways outta town. Place called Boot Hill, weren't it . . . ?'

The livery man was sweating now and couldn't get them through the big double-doors fast enough. He was so thrown by the veiled threat that he even forgot to charge them for the overnight stalling of their horses.

They managed to hold in their laughter till they cleared the edge of town.

The townswoman had been right; the farm looked like what it was – somewhere between a rock and a hard place.

Wire fences sagged on leaning posts, a couple were snapped clean off. There were weeds and a rusted pump and a well with a tumbledown shelter with missing shingles. The house was more shack than cabin, part log, part clapboard and a lot of these had been patched, some with old coal-oil tins cut up and nailed over the broken places. There was grass and a couple of stunted bushes growing on the roof which seemed to have a deep bow in the middle.

But there was a flash of verdant green around the back and Doyle and Tyrell moved their approach so they could get a better look. Vegetable-gardens, with pretty good crops of tomatoes, corn, potatoes, cabbage, carrots and other plants they couldn't readily identify from here.

There were a couple of women's fripperies flapping on the clothes'-line nearby, propped up with saplings that had forked ends. There was no sign of life but there was a rickety stable in a far corner that might have held a horse. They couldn't be sure because of the deep shadows and a partly closed door, so they turned back and approached from the front.

They dismounted at the gate, had trouble getting it open, and made their way through the weeds to the front door. Still no sign of life. Tyrell shrugged impatiently and rapped his hard knuckles on the plank door.

'Ma'am? You in there? Couple gentlemen here like to have a word with you . . .'

Nothing happened and the rancher was about to knock again when suddenly the door opened, dragging one corner, and they glimpsed a smallish woman in a long grey dress with a bonnet in place, her face half-turned away from them. Light-coloured hair showed beneath the bonnet and she wore gloves.

She put a hand up to her face, further hiding the features. The house behind her was dark and gloomy and Doyle realized with a shock that none of the windows were open. He wondered briefly how she found her way around in the darkness . . . .

'What do you want?'

Her voice was mellow but there was a hint of tightness in it, as if she didn't use it a lot.

Tyrell doffed his hat a shade late – Doyle already had his in his hands. He said:

'Would your name be "Claire", ma'am?'

'What if it is?' No real belligerence, but little interest, too.

'Well, we been,' Doyle started, but then a man's voice spoke from the darkness behind the woman.

'Let 'em in, Claire. Thought I recognized the voices.'

A man moved out of the shadows and Doyle made out the shotgun in his hands. Then he shifted his gaze to the man's face and was lost for words.

Not so Tyrell.

'Goddlemighty! Lang Dawson!'

'I've been called that – or 'Doc' Emmett. Depends where you knew me.'

The shotgun barrels jerked as the woman stepped to one side.

'Come on in, Matt. We're both a long ways from Blood Creek, here.'

103

9
The Box

In the parlour, Doc Dawson spoke to the girl in a low, intense voice for several minutes before she reluctantly opened the shutters on a window, quickly turning away and stepping back into the shadows.

Doyle frowned. She had made no effort to remove the bonnet or gloves and yet she showed no signs of going out. Then a little watery sunlight washed over her face briefly and he saw the reason she was wearing the bonnet.

It was only a glimpse, but he had seen the shine of scar tissue along her jaw and disappearing up under the light-coloured hair that had been drawn down over one ear. He didn't see the eye properly but had the impression of puckered flesh with no sign of an eyebrow.

The hands – well, he looked more closely now, and saw a little nest of scars showing above the gloves.

This young woman had been in some kind of terrible accident and she wore the scars on her face and hands. No wonder she avoided the townsfolk and tried to hide herself in the dark.

Matt Doyle immediately felt compassion for Claire. What hell it must be for a young woman to have to live like this! She had a good enough figure from what he could see of it, although the shapeless grey dress did nothing to show it off. The townswoman had said she was in her mid-twenties, his own age . . . She started to turn away and he glimpsed the other side of her face: the skin was smooth, unblemished and the good eye was a clear blue. *My God, she's beautiful!* he thought. *Half beautiful, anyway – poor kid . . . .*

She caught him staring and she gasped, tugged the bonnet closer and hurried from the room.

'Fire,' Doc Dawson said quietly. 'Married to a drunkard and a wife-beater. They had a boy child. Only months old – burned to death when the husband set fire to their cabin. She got them scars trying to save the kid.'

'What happened to the husband?' Doyle asked.

'Yellow bastard ran away – but I eventually caught up with him . . .' He paused. 'Claire was lucky to pull through. Been hidin' out ever since, ashamed to show her scarred face. She moves around a lot because folk are kind of leery and suspicious of anyone who don't conform and they spied on her a lot. Won't have a match or a lamp or candle in the place, don't even cook. You seen her garden. Eats nothin' but vegetables and drinks milk and water. Got a cow grazin' out there someplace . . . Been here a couple years or so now.'

'How come *you*'re here?' demanded Tyrell. 'They grant your appeal?'

Dawson sobered and shook his head. 'Kicked it out. Lousy judge said I had to serve another five years before I'd be eligible for parole. So I walked out.'

'Just like that!' Tyrell scoffed.

Dawson smiled crookedly. 'Actually, I crawled out, under the west wall – me and my cell-mate dug a tunnel.'

Doyle instinctively looked around the room and Dawson shook his head.

'Mort never made it. Guards caught him in the tunnel. Must've thought he was on his own, and then it caved in. I high-tailed it. Wasn't nothin' I could do for him.'

Tyrell pursed his lips, glanced at Doyle who said, 'Recollect you had a theory there was a way out under that west wall, Doc.'

'I was right. But, never mind that part. I've still got a few friends who keep me in touch with things and I hear there was some kinda fracas involvin' Ace Kelly – and you, Matt. And now I see you're here with Cash, I reckon my hunch must've been right: you got the watch and bein' the kind, trustin' beholden soul you are, you set out to find Claire and give it to her like you promised me you would.'

'More or less, Doc,' Doyle admitted, somehow uneasy in the presence of this man he had shared a cell with for so long in Blood Creek jail.

Dawson looked older than he remembered: drawn, gaunted way down, more angular. His eyes were sunken but they still commanded a man's attention as they had in prison. Deep, penetrating, cold as rim-ice on a mountain stream, or burning with hatred and menace as the mood took him. Not all that tall – in fact, Matt was a few inches taller – but there was a power that exuded from the man and although Tyrell tried to act tough, there was no doubt as to who was in charge in that dim room. Just as it had been in jail. Doc had been decent enough when he wanted something done but just the same you had better *get* it done – and *his* way, too . . . .

'You lied to me, Doc. That story you told me was just so much eye-wash.'

'Yeah, well, sorry I had to do it, but I knew you were pretty smart and needed a story that sounded right, had some details to it. Mebbe I lied a little – by omission. Fact is, I didn't know if I could trust you, Matt.'

'I'd've done anything for you, Doc, after the way you took care of me in there.'

Dawson nodded, seemingly genuinely regretful. 'I know that now, boy. Like I said, I'm sorry, but felt I had to do it.'

Doyle nodded curtly. 'I guess you did.'

The room filled slowly with silence and Dawson broke it, holding out a bony hand.

'I guess I'll take the watch now, Matt.'

'Hold up!' snapped Tyrell. 'It ain't yours!'

'Ain't anyone's, come to that,' Dawson said, 'so it might's well be mine – seein' as I'm the one knows what to do with it.'

Cash Tyrell frowned, slitting his eyes.

'Now how would you know that?' he scoffed.

Dawson smiled without mirth, tapped his temple.

'Always said readin' was the best thing a man could do to gain knowledge. And knowledge'll see you through 'most any situation, Cash. But you never did learn that. I've had plenty of time to study all kinds

107

of things. I took a bit of a shine to history and you know, amongst the books the warden bought in for me, was one on the story of Wells Fargo. Written by that hot-shot chief detective of theirs when he retired, Jim Hume. It was published five years ago and it included the raid on the Dodge City express office . . .'

'The one we pulled!'

Doc nodded. 'Hume said he'd like to devote his retirement to trackin' down the robbers. He listed what was taken, all that money we shared —'

'What about that damn iron box Asa grabbed?' Tyrell cut in. 'It must've been worth plenty, and the cunnin' ol' sonuver never let on what was in it.'

Dawson smiled. 'Well, you have to remember Asa was gettin' his own back on Wells Fargo for firin' him. But he'd had access to all the schedules and lading-bills. He knew what was in that box. And he knew how much it'd hurt 'em to lose it.'

'Well, what the hell was in it?'

Dawson hesitated, looking from one man to the other.

'A few dozen gold coins,' he said finally.

Tyrell snorted. 'Well, even if they were double eagles, they wouldn't've been worth anywheres near what the rest of us got as a share.'

'There was a set of dies, too.' Doc added quietly.

'Dies?' Tyrell looked at Doyle who remained silent, face deadpan.

'From the Denver mint where the coins in the box were struck. Don't keep askin' questions, Cash. I'll tell you if you gimme a chance.'

Tyrell shrugged, spread his hands, inviting Dawson to continue.

'The coins were to be shipped to California, all one hundred of 'em, each worth twenty-five dollars face value.'

'Well, shoot! I told you the whole kit-and-caboodle wouldn't be anywheres near our shares! How come ol' Asa was content to take that box? He was a shrewd old codger and he wouldn't make a mistake like that.'

'You finished?' Dawson snapped and Tyrell made placating gestures with his hands, put a finger across his lips to indicate he wouldn't interrupt again.

'I said on face value they were worth twenty-five bucks each – but they weren't meant for normal circulation as currency. They were special coins of pure gold, struck to commemorate the twenty-fifth anniversary of California being admitted to the Union.'

'Thought the Spanish settled it way back in the seventeen-hundreds?' Doyle said, staring down Dawson's cold look.

'They did, but the US squeezed the Spaniards out after a lot of trouble and even during the big gold rush of 'forty-nine, California still wasn't a state, wasn't officially granted statehood till eighteen-fifty. The governor out there in eighteen-seventy-five figured it was worth commemorating and commissioned the Denver mint to strike this special coin.'

'Which, like you said, ain't a coin at all!' growled Tyrell. 'Just what the hell've we got here, Dawson? You're losin' me!'

'No such luck! No one'd be loco enough to spend these coins even if they were given one. They were for special presentation and with only one hundred struck and the mint's dies in the package, that iron box is worth a small fortune. Those are *rare* coins, boys. Rarest of the rare and even more so if the dies are destroyed so's no more can be struck.'

'Or if the dies were *thought* to be destroyed,' Doyle offered lightly. 'A man could hand-strike a few more whenever he was short of *dinero* then.'

Dawson smiled thinly. 'You got an evil mind, Matt. That book of Hume's said it'd been estimated that just one of those special coins would be worth thousands of dollars each to a collector – and if the dies were up for sale? Well, a man could name his own price. Up in the tens of thousand apiece.'

They needed a minute to get their breath after Dawson's announcement.

'So ol' Asa outsmarted us all,' Tyrell murmured. 'He knew about the shipment from workin' for Wells Fargo and never let on! Crafty ol' bastard!'

Dawson said nothing, but he was watching Doyle. Matt seemed to be thinking things out, his lips moving slightly, and then he looked up sharply.

'How did Resnick find out?'

'Just naturally greedy. Must've got to thinkin' about that iron box and why Asa seemed satisfied to take it. Guess he tortured it out of Asa, not where the box is hid, but what's in it . . .'

'The watch . . . it can help find the box?'

'How the hell?' growled Tyrell irritably. 'It's a goddamn *watch*! Not a compass . . .'

'Cash – a watch can be used as a compass, too, but this is better'n a compass,' Dawson said with a tight

110

smile. 'It can lead us right to that iron box.'

'How? I've had the blamed thing in pieces and there ain't no map or instructions scratched on it anywhere. Even the hands won't move, like they been riveted on . . .'

'That's it, ain't it?' Doyle said abruptly. 'The position of the hands means something!'

Dawson smiled widely this time. 'You always were pretty smart at figurin' things, Matt. Yeah. Set the watch on the right map in the right place, and you'll find that box of coins.'

'Hell, *maps* now!' snapped Tyrell. 'We don't have no maps!'

'No, we don't,' admitted Dawson. 'But Claire does. See, this old farm once belonged to Asa Larkin. He only used that shack where we met him for shady deals and then he'd come back here, livin' like a hermit. The townsfolk, being like they are here, let him alone and he didn't bother them.'

'Where does Claire fit in?' Doyle asked quietly.

Dawson took his time answering.

'She's my daughter. She got scarred like I told you, hid away from the world, said no one would ever want her again, moved around a lot. Resnick got to Asa at his other place near St Jo and finished him, and the townsfolk didn't turn a hair when I sent Claire in here claiming she was Asa's daughter and a widow. She let 'em know she wanted to be left alone and went through Asa's things, found a couple hidey-holes and in one of 'em was a map of an old gold-mine that Asa used to work after Wells Fargo fired him. Map showed shafts drawn in, figures that meant nothin' to Claire.

But it had been well hid and wrapped up in oilskin so's it wouldn't be damaged, so she knew it *had* to mean something. And fact is, the mine's registered with the mines department as the *El Lobo Solo* mine – you know what that means in English?'

'Lone Wolf,' Doyle answered quietly.

'Just like the wolf embossed on the watch-case. Now,' he suddenly swung up the shotgun which the others had all but forgotten he was holding down at his side.

'Which one of you has the watch . . . ?'

'We've got 'em, boss!'

Kelly snapped his head up irritably from his account books once again as Grimm burst into his office. It was the first time that Ace Kelly could recall ever seeing the hardcase give a real, ear-to-ear smile. He strode briskly across the room and leaned his big scarred hands on the edge of the desk. The gash on his face was puckered now after it had been lanced by the doctor and drained of pus. Grimm disdained the idea of covering it with strip plaster and actually seemed quite proud to exhibit yet another scar.

'Followin' up on that riverboat paid off, boss!' he told Kelly a mite breathlessly. 'We think they went on board with a bunch of trailherders who were shippin' their broncs south . . .'

'You *think*?' Kelly was annoyed at the interruption, his head still full of figures as he tried to find just where his head barkeep was shaving the profits on booze deliveries. He had almost had it when Grimm came busting in and now he had to make a real effort to listen to the man. Anyway, he didn't like to be

112

proved wrong, and he had said he didn't believe Doyle and Tyrell would be stupid enough to take the river-boat. 'I need more than that, for Chrissakes!'

Grimm held up a hand. 'The trailherders quit here and there along the river – they were paid off and goin' home. The only two hosses left on board when the steamer pulled into New Madrid belonged to two rannies who sound one *helluva* like Doyle and Cash Tyrell.'

Kelly frowned. 'New Madrid? That's a long ways south. Why would they go all that far . . .' Suddenly he sat upright and Grimm straightened slowly, seeing the enlightenment wash across Kelly's face. 'Asa Larkin did some prospectin' of sorts down that way – across in Arkansas. Some old Spanish mine he talked about once. He opened it up and found a little gold but it petered out and then his pet bird died and I never heard him talk about it any more.'

Grimm frowned. 'He gave up because a damn bird died?'

'It died down the goddamn mine, you fool! He took it down in a cage to check the air was good. Lots of gases collect in them old mines, some explosive, others just plain poison. Coal-miners used canaries. Asa had this lousy-lookin' parrot with hardly any feathers. You ask me it likely died of old age as much as bad air. But – the hell with that. Point is, Asa worked that country, and I ain't thought about that mine in a coon's age.'

'You know where it is?'

Kelly's face straightened as he shook his head. 'No. He was full of that moonshine rotgut he used to make at the time. Never knew if he was talkin' sense or not

113

when he was like that. Never paid much attention to what he was sayin'.'

'Worth followin' up, you reckon?'

Kelly drew in a long breath, looked at the jumble of figures on his pad and sighed.

'We don't have anythin' else – and if you're sure Doyle and Tyrell left the riverboat there . . . ?'

Grimm felt his belly lurch. *Damnit! Kelly was doing it again! Putting it all on him so if anything went wrong Kelly wouldn't look the fool and he'd have someone to blame.*

'Descriptions seem to fit, boss . . .' he said lamely.

'OK. Send a couple of the boys down there, and we'll ride out. Be a helluva lot faster than takin' a river-steamer.' He shook his head. 'Let's hope you're right, Grimm. I'd hate to waste all that time.'

The hardcase nodded jerkily, muttering to himself as he hurried out.

Grimm chose to ride on ahead himself with another hardcase rather than stay back with Ace Kelly. The saloon-man would find more and more responsibility to push onto his shoulders and Grimm would have more and more to worry about . . . .

What he needed was to have something concrete to give to Kelly when he arrived.

Down as far as Cape Girardeau, he heard that the riverboat MS *Miss Abigail*, the same one Doyle and Tyrell rode down to New Madrid – *he hoped*! – was taking on passengers, preparing to sail the next morning on the 4 a.m. tide on its journey back up north.

With his two men, Curt Borlan and Chet Lea – the man he had hired to check out the riverboats – Grimm waited until all the commotion of loading was done and the passengers were eating the evening meal in the *Abigail*'s dining-salon, watching from the dock for the crew to come ashore. They would be allowed a few hours in town before the boat was ready to sail.

Grimm had already found out that the mate's name was Tallon and Chet Lea pointed out the burly, knot-fisted sailor wearing a seaman's battered cap. His shirt was open to the waist, showing a hairy chest with some South Seas tattoo design over the left breast.

'Hey, Tallon, got a minute?' Grimm called, staying in the shadows.

The mate swung along, arms dangling and swinging like a gorilla's, and half-turned his square head.

'Why?'

'Got a gold ten-dollar piece that could end up in your pocket, mebbe with some company . . .'

Tallon was wary as he approached the shadows and made out the shapes of three men.

'Cotter!' he bawled suddenly as a gangling man lurched by on his way uptown. 'C'mere!'

The man came across and when he saw the shadowy men he slipped a hand inside his shirt.

'What you want, Tal?'

'Just stand by . . .'

Grimm stepped forward confidently.

'On your last trip down river from St Louis . . . two men got off at New Madrid, with their hosses. Name of Doyle and Tyrell . . .' He paused to see if the mate would show any reaction but the big, scarred, broken-nosed face showed nothing except contempt for this cowboy. Grimm held up the small gold coin between his thumb and finger, flicking his gaze to Cotter who sucked in his breath noisily through broken teeth. 'This and maybe a friend if you can tell me where they were headed.'

'Tell you nothin',' Tallon growled. 'You loco enough to flash gold down at the docks, you deserve all you get. Cotter!'

Cotter moved swiftly, a hand going to the back of his neck and flicking out the knife that rested there in a flat sheath. It flashed dully as it sped through the night and buried itself to the hilt in the throat of Chet Lea even as the man hauled out his sixgun. He went down, choking, spraying blood.

The sight of his pard dying like this threw Curt Borlan out and although he triggered his Colt the bullet was wild. Grimm reacted as he always did – fast and deadly. He dropped to one knee and his gun came up blazing, his left hand chopping at the hammer, flame lancing the night like daggers of lightning. Cotter lurched and staggered, trying to throw a second knife he had drawn and a third bullet took away his lower jaw. By that time, Tallon was stumbling back with a bullet in the shoulder and another through the chest. He went down with blood gurgling in the back of his throat.

Before he hit the ground, Grimm kicked him in the side and stretched him out, kneeling on the wounded chest, the hot muzzle of his gun pressed up beneath the man's ear that had a golden-wire ring through the mangled lobe.

Grimm ripped the ring free, tearing away more flesh and Tallon screamed as the blood flowed down his sun-wrinkled neck. Grimm wasn't worried about anyone coming: the dock was well outside of town, on a promontory of land where the water was deeper, for one thing, and the passengers in the dining-salon were being entertained by the steamboat company's brass band.

'Guess you don't need the money, Tallon, but I still need that information. Feel like talkin'?'

Tallon did – but it was mostly obscenities and salty insults. Grimm sighed, groped around and found the wound in Tallon's chest. The man stopped in mid-curse. Then he began to scream as Grimm forced his fingers in the hole and began to tear it open. The mate convulsed under him and thrashed wildly, head rolling in unbearable pain. Grimm eased up some because he felt even the brass band might not mask Tallon's screams.

As the mate's bloody chest heaved and the breath roared and bubbled in his throat, hissed raggedly through flattened nostrils, Grimm said amiably:

'You're in fine voice, Tallon. Want to try for drownin' out the brass band? I reckon I can get you up to yelling loudly enough . . . .'

He lowered his head as Tallon's bloody mouth worked as he said a few hoarse words.

'What's that, *amigo*? Speak up or I'll have to do somethin' to make you talk louder.'

'Calico – Creek! Friend o' mine was in – Pocohontas when – they came. Young'un asked – way to Calico – Creek!'

'Mmmmm. You tryin' for that ten bucks now, or you just talkin' so's I won't massage that wound?' To emphasize his words, Grimm slammed the heel of his

117

hand onto the wound and Tallon convulsed and almost passed out. 'How – did – your – friend – come – to tell – you – this? Pocohontas is a long ways from the Big Muddy.'

Tallon fought for breath and his words were slurred and sentences broken, but Grimm finally put it together. The mate's pard had got into a little trouble over a woman – somone else's woman, of course – and he had had to leave Pocohontas in a hurry. Broke, he picked up a job on the *Abigail*, which was still unloading and taking on cargo for ports to the south before turning back north. In the course of general conversation he had mentioned that two of *Abigail*'s passengers who had disembarked at New Madrid had come through Pocohontas . . . .

Grimm accepted the explanation: it sounded genuine enough and Tallon was almost weeping with pain and expecting more. Curt Boland had been kneeling beside Chet Lea's body, now he looked around at Grimm. 'Chet's gone!'

Grimm ignored the remark. 'Grab this one's feet. See if he can swim with that lead in him or if it'll make him sink.'

'Judas, Grimm, you sure Ace wanted this kinda mess?'

'Got what we wanted didn't we? Grab them feet!'

Tallon struggled feebly and yelled all the way until the splash drowned out his cries and his mouth filled with muddy water. Grimm stood on the bank, leaned out a little.

'Aw, shoot! He's gone under. Was hopin' for a little target practice.'

118

10
Decoys

Doc Dawson played it close to his chest.

Once he had the watch and had taken the guns from Doyle and Tyrell, he made them sit on the old sofa with its busted springs.

'All the way back,' he ordered, gesturing with the shotgun. 'Sit all the way back!'

They did and felt their buttocks sink deep into an area where the rawhide slinging and springs had collapsed. They were effectively stymied even if they decided to make a lunge for Dawson. Sitting as they were, knees high towards their chests because of the collapsed support, they would have no chance – they would have to struggle and flounder and by that time Dawson could shoot them or gun-whip them unconscious, maybe even taking time to roll a cigarette before he made a move.

The girl had come back and she watched them closely but she did not seem to be armed. Dawson laid the shotgun – one hammer cocked – on the scarred

119

table, took a folded paper from a drawer in the side-board. This was the old map, apparently, and it had torn on the creases but someone, likely the girl, had pasted it to another sheet of paper to give it strength and more durability.

Dawson leered briefly at his prisoners, took out the watch, searched the map and found what he was look-ing for just below half-way down the right hand side of the map. He laid the watch on the paper, slid it across, and turned it this way and that, until his frown disap-peared and he smiled, glancing at his daughter.

'I was right, Claire! The watch hands show the way!'

She nodded but did not speak, nor take her gaze, from under the bonnet, off the men on the sofa. Dawson spoke to them.

'Old Asa was smarter than anyone gave him credit for. But I've worked it out now and I'm goin' to go get the iron box. Claire, you stay here with these gents. We'll tie 'em up before I leave. You can turn 'em loose after dark if you want. I'll be long gone and they won't pick up any tracks before daylight, if then. You know where to meet me. And when.'

'Be careful down the mine, father. It smells – funny.'

'Methane most likely, but I'll watch it. I'll take Tonto to make sure.'

She stiffened. 'Not Tonto! No, you said you'd use another one!'

'No time, my dear – I'm on the run, if you recall and I need a stake, a big stake, for us to get away to South America . . .'

'But Tonto's my companion!' She was so upset that she forgot to keep her head lowered and once again

120

Doyle glimpsed the good side of her face. She had been truly beautiful: what a hell of a thing to be scarred-up that way.

'I'll get you another! Maybe even a bird.' Dawson spoke curtly now, folding the map. 'Hell, they've got big, colourful ones in South America – called macaws. You'll love 'em . . .'

She went from the room and came back hesitantly, carrying a narrow wire cage with a small grey squirrel in it, busily stuffing some leafy green vegetable into its mouth, tiny paws working swiftly.

'I've put some food in for him and water. Please see he gets plenty of fresh water.'

Dawson smiled as he took the cage from Claire who seemed reluctant to let it go. The squirrel hopped and climbed about the wire, chattering.

'She saved it, you know. Someone tied it up in a tree by its tail, kid most likely. It had a busted leg and there was a storm comin' up – she climbed the tree and brought it down, splinted the leg, and nursed it through.' He shrugged, holding up the cage to look at the tiny animal. 'OK, Tonto. Time to pay back all that attention and care you've had.'

'Please don't let him die, father!' Claire's voice was steady but the one eye that Doyle could see was pleading. 'As soon as he shows signs of distress, take him back to where the air is clean . . . Promise me!'

'Sure, honey, I promise. You know me.' He picked up the watch and map, put them into his pockets and then lifted the shotgun, the barrels swinging casually towards his prisoners. 'Now lie down on the floor on your faces and put your hands behind your back.

121

Claire, fetch that rope from the kitchen and tie 'em up. I'm rarin' to go collect our fortune!'

'That mean you're not cuttin' us in?' asked Tyrell as the girl went to work on his wrists with the rope.

Dawson laughed. 'You got more of a sense of humour than I figured, Cash!'

'You son of a bitch! You wouldn't have that watch now, 'cept for me!'

'Wrong, Cash. It was Matt got the watch for me. Knew he would track it down eventually. He's still a mite green but someone brung him up right, taught him that when you're beholden, you square the debt at any cost. And I made sure he was beholden to me.'

Doyle managed to turn his head and look up at Dawson.

'You know, Doc, you look a lot smaller out here in the real world than you did running things in Blood Creek.'

Dawson didn't like that, but forced a grin.

'Hell, boy, I saved your ass – literally. Motives don't matter, now do they? It's the act that counts.'

Doyle nodded, tight-lipped as the girl began tying rope around his wrists.

'Well, *adios*, fellers. I s'pect you'll come after me but I'll be long gone – and South America's a big place they tell me. I don't figure we'll ever meet again.'

'You better hope we don't,' murmured Tyrell, but Dawson ignored him, kissed the girl lightly on the good side of her face and hurried from the room.

Just before sundown the girl returned with a tray bearing two platters of salad and two glasses of milk and a

122

slab of cheese. She set the tray down on the table, returned to the kitchen and when she came back she had a knife in one hand and a heavy Colt .45 in the other.

The two men, hands bound, had each been placed in an easy chair and she now stood between these chairs, looking at them in the room that was filled with a ruby glow as the sun sank below the rim of the hills out towards the badlands.

Her face was still in the shadow of the bonnet.

'I'm sorry if you're not used to fresh food and only milk to drink but it's all I have. Now I'm going to release one of you and he can untie the other's hands. I'll watch while you eat.' She indicated the gun. 'I can use this. I'm quite a good shot and the range here is – well, very close.'

'What would you want to shoot us for, sweetheart?' asked Tyrell with a false smile. 'We ain't gonna give you no trouble.'

'I know,' she said confidently, walked behind Doyle's chair and severed the ropes binding him. 'I hate cutting good rope but under the circumstances . . .'

He rubbed his wrists briskly until he could feel his hands and fingers and then worked on Tyrell's knots. He glanced up at the girl as he did so.

'Think Tonto'll survive?'

She jumped a little and he knew he had been right in surmising that the squirrel's fate was uppermost in her mind. She was a very *young* woman in her thinking, almost childlike: no doubt the ordeal of the fire had something to do with it.

'Those mines are tricky. Seems mostly good air then

suddenly there's a pocket of bad.'

Her head snapped towards him. 'You know mines?'

'I've been in 'em,' he temporized, remembering a time when he and Jigger Bush had hidden in a deep-shaft mine to escape a posse. (*Those were good days, Jigger! Or we thought they were. Rest easy, old pard!*) Yeah, they had to grope their way blindly through tunnels, eventually found a way out onto a steep talus slope, mostly mine tailings. They had passed two bodies inside the mine and found a third man in a hell of a state at the foot of the slope. He told them about the bad air inside and how lucky they were to have escaped it. (They had looked upon it as *fun!*) To this day he didn't know how it had happened but later they heard that a posse man had been looking for them in that same mine. He had carried a storm lantern and there had been an explosion that had brought down half the mountain. Gases were blamed . . . .

'Father promised he would take care of Tonto,' she said doggedly but, Doyle thought, not with a lot of conviction. 'He always keeps his word to me.'

'What happens now?' Tyrell asked, rubbing his hands as he sat down at the table, obviously hungry. Doyle joined him and began to eat a leaf of lettuce and a carrot.

'You're free to leave after you've eaten. You'll never find father before he finds the box.'

'What about you, Claire?' Doyle asked.

'I know what to do.'

The room grew darker as they ate swiftly, drank the milk. The meal was surprisingly satisfying.

'What about our guns?' Tyrell asked.

'You'll find them with your horses in the trees down by the creek. Go left but be careful making your way in the dark – it's tricky and there's a lot of trash and gopher holes. The horses are on this side of the creek.'

Tyrell grabbed his hat and nudged Doyle who was sitting at the table. 'Let's go.'

'In a minute. Claire, I spent a lot of time with your father in jail. He was good to me. But he used me all the time. I was so green that I never realized it before.'

'He had a right. You were beholden to him.'

'Sure – I'm still grateful to him. But – I think he's used you, too, and will again.'

She stiffened and the sixgun covered him. 'I don't care what you think! He's my father.'

Doyle smiled thinly. 'And you feel beholden, too.'

She was breathing heavily now. 'He – he provided for me! Plenty of parents wouldn't bother with – someone who looks like me.'

'Plenty *would*.'

'Oh! Just – *go*! Both of you. *Now*!'

They left and heard her lock the door after them. It was not quite dark but they still had trouble finding their mounts: she had given them wrong directions. The horses were on the far bank, to the right and upstream. They had to wade across. Their guns were there, but unloaded. By then the stars were blazing in a jet-black sky.

'Smart girl,' Doyle commented, thumbing home cartridges into his Colt's chambers.

'Little bitch ain't so smart,' Tyrell growled, swearing as he dropped some cartridges in the pitch darkness.

'She's goin' to meet Doc. All we gotta do is follow

her.' It sounded easy – and logical.

Only thing was, when they finally found their way out of the trees and back to the cabin and checked, the girl was no longer there.

'Pretty smart like I said,' Doyle allowed and, strangely, feeling quite pleased about it. 'She lit out while we've been stumbling around down by the creek.'

Ace Kelly was not in a good mood – a chronic state of affairs lately, it seemed.

He hadn't ridden so far nor for so long for many months and his back ached, his spine felt as if it had a knot in it half-way down to his butt and his head throbbed. To add to the general bad feeling he was still riled over his head barkeep back in St Louis.

He hadn't yet figured out how the man was stealing from his profits. He almost had it when Grimm arrived with the news about Doyle and Cash Tyrell. Somehow he had lost the thread and then it was time to start riding south. He hated leaving such unfinished business but he knew he would settle things when he got back. And the longer he had to wait, the more brutal that settlement would be – Grimm and his sidekick, Bud Lynn, would see to that.

Now, riding through rain that was getting heavier by the minute, Kelly figured he'd better concentrate on catching up with Doyle and Tyrell. *That* was where the big money lay! Money that would soon be his.

With the pace he had set, the other men riding with him complaining amongst themselves, they ought to reach Calico Creek by sundown tomorrow.

*

Tyrell was fit to be tied.

'That little bitch! How the hell we gonna find her now?'

'Maybe she hasn't gone anywhere,' Doyle said slowly. 'Remember she won't use a light or anything with a naked flame. She could still be in there.'

It stopped Tyrell in mid-curse as they crouched by the cow bale, the smell of manure strong.

'There's no hoss in the stable,' Tyrell said savagely.

'I'm gonna look inside anyway.'

Doyle made for the house and against his better judgement, Tyrell followed. The door was locked. They tried poking a clasp-knife blade through the keyhole but couldn't force the lock. Then Tyrell, impatient, worked his fingers in around a warped shutter on the kitchen window and strained and pulled and sweated until it came free – making the devil of a racket.

No sound from inside and Doyle climbed in, worried that Tyrell in his present mood might shoot at the first noise inside and wound or even kill the girl. There was no key in the locked door so Tyrell climbed in after him but a quick search revealed no sign of Claire.

'Damn! She's lit a shuck!'

'Seems like it,' Doyle agreed, lighting a match and making his way into the parlour. He lit other matches and went to the sideboy. He had noticed other papers in the drawer where Dawson had got his map. He found a second map but it was obviously much smaller-scale than the one Dawson had used.

127

'Hold it!' Doyle said as Tyrell made to shake out his match. 'Light another.' He spread out the map and studied it quickly. It showed Calico County, the town, the dried-out salt lake and the ranges. Also the area that had been mined many years earlier, in the general direction of the hills.

Doyle tapped that part of the map.

'This is where the Spaniards made the Indians work for gold. Some of the old mines've been reopened over the years from time to time but no one got rich far as I know.'

'So?'

'The mines are marked. Names on some – *El Lobo Solo* pencilled in.

Tyrell shouldered him aside and looked.

'But this ain't the map Doc used.' Tyrell sounded ◀ suspicious, as if Doyle was trying to trick him in some way.

'No, smaller scale. He used one where he could fit the watch. Must've had some numbers or directions on it to line up with the way Larkin left the hands set. Doc took that map with him, but this one'll give us a general direction.'

'Gal says he'll be long gone.'

Doyle smiled. 'You ever been down one of them real old mines? Shafts and tunnels running in all directions. Ladders and shoring rotten – easy as hell to get lost, or have an accident. And Doc's an amateur. Told me in jail he'd never been down a mine, just never had the urge nor the need.'

'Then we forget the gal. Go straight to the mine area and hope Doc's still there . . .'

Doyle nodded. 'Have a feeling he will be. The gal, too.'

Tyrell frowned. 'She'll be ridin' to where she's s'posed to meet him, won't she?'

'Might – but I figure she'll go to the mine first. To check on the squirrel if for no other reason.'

Tyrell looked his disbelief, jaw hanging open.

'You're joshin'!'

'How much you want to bet? Half of what's in that iron box, maybe . . .?'

'Yeah,' Tyrell said slowly and he was smirking when Doyle looked up in surprise. 'Yeah – *your* half!'

Doyle's instincts saved him. He didn't see Tyrell draw his gun because the man let the match fall and stood on it. Instantly, Doyle dropped flat, rolling away across the floor, snatching at his own sixgun as Tyrell's roared, the muzzle-flash throwing the small untidy room into momentary relief and detail. Tyrell's moving body knocked over a chair.

The lead tore and gouged the floor, splinters flying. Doyle twisted onto his belly as Tyrell triggered twice more. Matt fired simultaneously with the last shot but felt the impact of lead as a bullet slammed into him, kicking his body against the wall.

Tyrell shot twice more, lunging to one side, firing whilst in mid-air. Doyle moaned, got off another shot and then the gun fell from his hand, too heavy to hold . . . .

Cash Tyrell laughed even as his gun hammer clicked on an empty chamber.

'Green as a celery-stick, kid! I done you a favour. You were gonna get yourself killed anyway. I just saved you prolongin' the agony! So long, sucker!'

He groped for a match, snapped it into flame on his thumbnail and looked down at the still, bloody body huddled against the wall.

'Too bad, kid – for you.'

Tyrell grunted, scooped up the crumpled map from the table and made his way back to the kitchen, first tossing the still-burning match onto an overturned easy chair with stuffing hanging out of a rent in the fabric covering.

It smouldered briefly before bursting into flame.

11
Fire!

Doyle awoke coughing, his face seared by a great heat on one side.

He didn't know where he was at first and then, as the roaring of the dancing flames crowded into his brain, he remembered how Tyrell had tried to kill him. He grunted as he moved, deep pain in his right side just above his trousers belt. *Likely that meant some sort of serious wound!* There was more pain, but not so bad, alongside his head, and he felt the stickiness of blood down one side of his face, the side turned away from the fire.

The parlour was ablaze. What furniture there had been was rapidly consumed as it was mainly old dried-out wood. Even as he squinted through the smoke and began to cough again, feeling as if his lungs were tearing apart inside his chest, the dining-table collapsed and showered him with sparks. His shirt began to smoulder and he beat at it feebly with his right hand, feeling again that deep, knifing agony in his side. He tried to roll away but slammed into the wall. Something under him hurt his hip and he groped

131

quickly, found his sixgun, automatically rammed it into his holster.

By that time, his brain was screaming at him: *Get the hell out of here!*

Doyle knew enough about fire to stay close to the floor: there was usually clearer air there, not entirely smoke-free, of course, but better than a foot above where the raw smoke swirled and seared a man's eyes as if it would prise them out of his head. It was mighty painful to move, and there was pooled blood on the floor where he had lain, but he managed to get his legs bent under him, pushed up with his arms.

That right side threatened to bring about his collapse with its onset of pain but he gritted his teeth, tears blinding him, as he groped his way slowly forward, towards where he could see the vague shape of a door.

Unfortunately, he chose the front door and it was locked. Even the metal handle burned his palm and he cried aloud in a brief curse, hung his head as his body was racked with a spasm of coughing. The old drapes had burned through by now and the ceiling was popping, hung down in one part, the sod and flowers spilling into the room and actually extinguishing the flames where they landed.

He floundered across, glimpsed the door leading to the kitchen as more roof gave way and poured a massive mound down, blocking the front door entirely. *If he hadn't moved when he had . . . .*

Doyle sobbed with effort, dragging himself through into the kitchen. It, too, was blazing and he crawled and made awkward swimming movements as he tried to reach the door leading to the outside. There were crashes all around now as the ancient timbers literally exploded and the walls caved in, tilting perilously. Huge gusts of searing heat battered him flat and filled his lungs with raw smoke. He coughed constantly, butted his head against a wall – the *outside* wall! He must be near the door, reached up blindly, feeling with blistered fingers for the handle.

He found it and while it was hot, he was able to hang on and turn it downwards. It was locked. He remembered then that they had been unable to unlock it and had had to come in via a window with a warped shutter that Tyrell had forced. Time was running out. A few minutes more and he would collapse from lack of air and then he would be cooked like a round-up steak that had fallen into the camp-fire.

His seeking fingers touched the window sill and he roared in pain as he pulled himself to his knees, his right side seeming to tear apart. But he held his position, pushed at the shutter.

It wouldn't move. Tyrell must've wedged it closed before he had run off and left him to die here . . . .

Well, it looked like the rancher was going to get his wish. His brain felt as if it was cooking inside his skull as he slumped; back against the hot timber of the wall, flames leaping and writhing all round him.

What a helluva way to go! was his last thought as his chin slumped onto his chest and a furnace-blast set even the soles of his boots asmoking . . . .

That was when he passed out completely.

The grass under him was damp and the air was cool

and there were wet rags draped over his face and wrapped about his hands. He started to remove them, shaking his head so as to dislodge the towel or whatever it was from his face and that crippling pain tore through his right side once more.

The house had collapsed into a pile of still-burning timbers but the fire was dying slowly, the glow a deep, dull amber. He had to think back through pain and a crashing headache and the rawness of smoke in his lungs that felt as if it was peeling the skin from the back of his throat.

Must've gotten that door open after all.

But God knew how! He had felt so weak – still had no more strength than a new-born babe. But somehow he must've opened that door and rolled over the stoop and away from the burning shack . . . .

And where had the wet towels and cloths come from?

The thought crashed through his semi-comatose state.

It brought him wide awake. How the hell! Someone must've covered him with the towels. Townsfolk? No, they might've seen the glow but it was too far out for them to worry much about it, going on their earlier attitude . . . .

The roaring and piercing noises in his ears faded after a while and it was during one of these lulls when the flames were dying and no longer making crackling sounds, that he heard something in the rickety stables. *But there had been no horse in there when he and Tyrell had arrived!*

Something moved down there even as he slowly and painfully turned his head. A shadow stepped out of the darkness of the stables and he groped for his sixgun, trying to recall if it still had any cartridges in the chambers . . . .

His hands were blistered and cut and he was way too slow. Whoever it was came hesitantly, warily, held something or, more like, *brandished* whatever weapon it was. He thought he was in for a cracked skull. At least.

Then the newcomer stopped, staring down at him and he heard rasping breath and a voice that almost stopped his heart said:

'Are you – all right – Mr Doyle? I – I just dragged you over the stoop and let you fall – then – *ran* and hid in the stables ... I'm sorry if – I made your injuries worse.'

Must be dreaming – Have *to be dreaming!*

It was Claire Dawson who had rescued him from the blazing shack.

There was grey light showing in the east now and Matt Doyle sat against a corner of the draughty stables, his wounds bandaged, wearing a fresh shirt the girl had fetched from his saddle-bags. He was surprised Tyrell had left his horse but the man was likely moving fast and eager to be a long way from the blazing shack by the time he reached the tethered mounts.

The severe, knifing pain in Doyle's right side, which he feared might be a mortal wound, turned out to be something more mundane. It was a three-inch sliver of wood, torn up from the shack's floorboards by one of Tyrell's first bullets. The girl had removed it, painfully but successfully. The second wound was a graze on the side of his head and apart from losing a little hide and hair – and giving him a thundering headache – it was little to worry about.

The girl hunkered down a few feet from him, her gloves burned near the fingertips and the edge of the bonnet charred. There were also burn-holes in her dress. Doyle set his eyes upon her silent form in the dim light – she no longer seemed to care if he saw her full-face now, but she would not remove the dirty bonnet.

'How come?' he rasped, throat still raw from the smoke. 'I mean – the fire. You – dragged me out . . .'

She remained silent for a time and then said, after a deep sigh:

'I – was in the trees, watching, when you and Tyrell arrived. I'd locked up the shack to make it look as if I had left.'

'Why?'

'To see if you had remembered seeing the second map and would come back for it.' He frowned and she almost smiled. 'It was a decoy, of course. Father is an intelligent man as I expect you know. He knew once you were free and in the dark and you thought I'd left to rendezvous with him that you'd either wait till daylight in an effort to find my tracks and follow me – or *you* would be the one to remember seeing the second map in that drawer.' She sobered abruptly. 'We – I – didn't expect Tyrell to try and kill you . . .'

'Me neither,' he said grimly.

'After the shooting I watched him wedge the shutter closed in the kitchen and as he rode out I saw the first flames. I – wanted to run away, actually mounted my horse – but . . .'

She went quiet and he held back, not prompting her, figuring she would explain in her own way and in her own good time.

'I – couldn't leave. I – I'd failed once to rescue – someone from a – fire . . .' Her bosom was heaving with her emotion and her voice trembled slightly. 'I – saw this as a second chance – a test. To – try to conquer my fear and – perhaps save your life.'

'You didn't know if I was dead or alive.'

'No. I told myself you were probably dead – I think I hoped you were and then, of course, I wouldn't have to go near the burning shack. I – compromised with myself. I had the key to the back door – the front was already burning – and I decided I'd unlock it and – push it open – leave a way out for you if – you were still alive.'

Another pause, a long deep breath.

'I saw you huddled beneath the window – just a few feet away. The flames were already licking out from the doorway. You *moved*! If you hadn't jerked and coughed, I'd've – run . . .'

'But you didn't. You dragged me out and doctored me and I'm almighty grateful, Claire.' He smiled faintly. 'Once again I'm beholden to the Dawsons.'

She snapped her head up.

'No! No, don't feel that way – I had – something to make up for – that other fire – I'm – content – that I've done so. I want no other reward, nor anyone feeling beholden to me . . .'

He smiled fully now. *She was sure some gal!*

'You don't have anything to blame yourself for in that other fire. It's obvious you tried your damndest to get the boy out.'

137

She lifted her face to him and he saw it clearly for the first time, the scarred left side, neatly divided from the unblemished right profile by the pert little nose.

'Not everyone sees my scars in that way, Matt Doyle!'

'Because they don't know you.'

She made a small sound; he realized it was a brief laugh.

'And you do? In such a short time?'

'Yeah. You risked your own life to save me, went into a situation that utterly terrified you – and you did it. You dragged me free. Now it's time to come to terms with it, Claire. You don't need to live in darkness any more.'

She sobered. 'I don't intend for people to stare at me, make fun of the way I look!'

'Cover up like you've been doing, sure, but don't make a hermit of yourself. Anyway, aren't there doctors who can help? I seem to recollect Doc reading a thick book in jail about some doctor in a place called Vienna who worked with folks' own skin, took some from one part of the body and grew it over a scarred part. As I recall he was damned excited about it, but he never discussed it. Of course I didn't know about you then . . .'

'I've – heard of such things but the men who work that way are in Europe or somewhere. Too far away and much too costly . . .' She sighed again in that characteristic way, lifting the small shoulders, head tilting slightly as she sighed, looking forlorn. 'I dare say I'll work up enough courage one day to walk down the street with my head erect and – unafraid.'

'I'd be proud to walk by your side if you need someone to kind of boost your confidence.'

Claire looked at him sharply, the left eye with the hooded lid glinting briefly.

'That's kind of you, but I don't think that'll be for a long, long time – if ever.'

'Claire, you beat that fire and you saved my life. You can walk anywhere with your head erect. Just don't leave it too long before you do it.'

'We'll see. What will you do now?'

He knew she was deliberately changing the subject.

'Guess I can ride, so I'll go see if I can find Tyrell and your father . . . No, wait – you said that map was fake. Which means Cash'll be a long way from the real location of the *El Lobo Solo*. So, if you're going to Doc, I'd like to ride along.'

The girl seemed to think about it for quite some time. Then she stood, looking past the heap of smouldering timbers, small gloved hands clenching.

'Some people are coming out from town! Mostly to rubberneck, I suppose! Nobody turned up last night when they might've helped!' This last was said bitterly and when she saw Doyle struggling to get on his feet she went to help him. He saw five people, three in a buckboard and two riding double on a horse coming over the rise.

'You don't need folk like this, Claire! Let's get out of here.'

'Are you sure you can ride?'

He grinned, trying to hide the pain he felt.

'If I fall off, you can help me get back into the saddle. I wouldn't even try to ride unless someone was with me.'

139

He deliberately put her in a position where her conscience would dictate her next move. He saw her mouth tighten; she didn't like being manipulated like that but she nodded, took his arm and helped him towards the tree line where the horses were.

Even after only a few steps, Doyle, already gasping and faltering, wondered about his sanity in attempting to ride so soon.

Cash Tyrell kicked at the rotten log near where he had ground hitched his horse. The soggy wood spewed out in a fan of harmless splinters and he cussed angrily, totally frustrated.

He had checked out three mines as marked on the map he had taken from Dawson's shack – and none of them was any goddamn *good*! In the first, *El Lobo Solo*, the drive-tunnel had collapsed long ago, and filled the entrance from floor to dripping ceiling. He found a rusted cap-and-ball Colt Navy pistol embedded in the pile and knew the place hadn't been worked for twenty years.

The second was little better: he had reached the second level and then the rotten ladder had given way, leaving him suspended by his hands over an apparently bottomless pit of darkness. He was lucky to make it back to solid ground. He had smoked three cigarettes before he felt up to tackling the next shaft.

It went nowhere, ended against a wall of solid rock showing not one speck of ore-bearing quartz. By now it had sunk in that he had taken a deliberately mismarked map.

Just like that son of a bitch Doc Dawson! Well, he

had struck out and all it meant was he had been a fool. Now he didn't know *where* the hell to look . . . .

But the problem was about to be solved for him.

A shot cracked at the same moment that a bullet chewed a fist-sized chunk out of the rotted log, spraying him with soggy wood. As he stumbled and reached for his sixgun, a second shot thunked into the log and a voice he knew only too well called:

'Just stay put, Cash! Or the next one'll take your head off!'

Half a dozen horsemen came down out of the rocks half-way up the slope and his stomach hit his boots: Ace Kelly, Grimm and a bunch of hardcases who would rather beat a man to death than eat. Kelly thumbed back his sweat-stained hat.

'By God, we've had a lo-o-o-ong, hard ride, Cash, *amigo*, and I'm here to tell you I ain't in any mood for joshin'. So don't waste my time. Which mine is the one Asa Larkin worked?'

Grimm and Bud Lynn dismounted and came and stood either side of the grey-faced Tyrell. Kelly leaned forward, in the saddle, cupping one hand behind an ear.

'I can't hear you!'

'I – I been four-flushed, Ace! They gimme a fake map.'

'*Goddamnit!* I told you no flim-flam! I ain't in the mood! Grimm, Bud . . .'

Tyrell started to protest but Grimm kicked him in back of the knees, and his legs folded. He started to fall and Bud Lynn sank a boot into his midriff. As Tyrell writhed on the ground, Lynn unsheathed his hunting-knife.

Grimm placed a boot across the gagging Tyrell's neck and Lynn stooped over him, the blade slicing away part of the struggling rancher's shirt, showing his white belly.

Then just as the cold steel touched his cringing flesh there was a low rumbling sound and the entire mountain seemed to tremble from an explosion deep within.

12
El Lobo Solo

The girl was reluctant at first to take him to the real *El Lobo Solo*, but watching him and seeing he was struggling to stay in the saddle, she decided there could be no real harm in it.

Doyle wasn't hurt quite as bad as he made out. His exhibition of obvious weakness was for Claire's benefit, to gain her sympathy, but mostly it was for Doc Dawson's benefit. She would tell her father just how weak he was on the ride out here, how he didn't appear dangerous . . . .

How that would affect Doc Dawson Doyle didn't know, but right now he didn't even know what Dawson had in mind for him. Clearly, he had meant Tyrell and Doyle to take the decoy map and lose themselves amongst the long-abandoned mines, while he rendezvoused with the girl, hopefully with Asa Larkin's iron box. But how he would react when she showed up with Doyle in tow was anyone's guess.

It was also clear that Claire, too, was uncertain, not even having thoroughly convinced herself that she had

143

done the right thing by bringing Doyle along.

But it was too late now. There was the mine entrance, showing low down in the side of a hill with a large pyramid of tailings nearby. Dawson's chestnut was ground hitched under a tree, its foliage shading a small waterbutt and a burlap sack that no doubt contained oats or grain.

A man who would leave his mount food and water in case something happened to him while he was underground, couldn't be all bad, Doyle allowed.

'Oh, he must've taken Tonto with him!' the girl said, dismounting quickly and running to the chestnut which had raised its head and given a short whinny when the riders arrived. She absently stroked the animal's muzzle, her face shaded by the charred bonnet. But Doyle knew her eyes were darting everywhere, looking for the caged squirrel.

Doyle almost fell off his horse and clung to the saddle horn to get his breath, the pain in his side stabbing, his head spinning. She saw him and hurried across taking one arm.

'I'm OK. Just got down a mite quick.'

Her blue eyes searched his face and she said quietly, 'He must still be inside – that's why Tonto's not here.'

He heard the tension in her voice.

'He gave you his word that he won't let anything happen to it,' Doyle said without conviction. He had always had the impression that Doc Dawson didn't care much one way or t'other about animals. 'Why don't we go find him?'

She nodded, held his arm as she led the way up the slope towards the mine entrance.

144

They were almost level with it when there came a dull, prolonged thunder from deep in the earth and Doyle staggered as the ground beneath his feet moved. The girl stumbled too, putting down her hands to steady herself. A gust of hot, dust-and-gravel-laden wind blasted out of the tunnel, whipping their clothes about them, stinging their eyes, knocking them flat.

They rolled back down the slope and tangled at the bottom. They could still hear crashes and falling rock through the ringing in their ears as they sat up. The girl's bonnet had come loose and he saw for the first time her golden-wheat hair and had a clear view of the scarred face. But she didn't care: she was looking wide-eyed up the slope to the entrance where dust still roiled, and cried, hoarsely, 'Father! *Father!*'

Doyle stood unsteadily, took her arm.

'Come on,' he said and began to lead her up the slope, wondering what they would find inside . . . .

That had been one hell of an explosion.

They couldn't see. They couldn't breathe, the pall of still-swirling dust was so thick inside the entrance. Doyle dragged the girl back as she tried to fight the choking cloud but was convulsed with a fit of coughing.

Outside they waited, both coughing, fighting for breath, doubled over. Doyle led her to some rocks and they sat down and she automatically adjusted her bonnet, which was jammed at an awkward angle at the back of her head, held by the ribbon tie. Matt Doyle hesitated a moment, then lent a hand – and she did not object, but she pulled the bonnet into place and tied the ribbon beneath her chin again. She looked at him quickly, then just as quickly averted her gaze.

'Best give it time to clear,' he said.

She stiffened. 'But – he might be lying – hurt!'

He nodded. 'Could be. But we can't even breathe in there. We'd end up two more casualties to no purpose.'

After a moment she nodded, lips compressed.

'All right. That makes sense.'

It took most of half an hour before the dust began to settle. Doyle had gone to the entrance several times but it had been too full of dust and debris to risk trying to penetrate the partly collapsed entrance tunnel. As he limped back to where she waited, poised on the rock, ready to leap to her feet, he shook his head slowly.

'Another ten minutes I reckon we'll get in . . .'

Then they heard the riders, *saw* them coming over the mountain above them. And coming fast! Six or seven, Doyle thought, snatching his sixgun, automatically checking the cylinder. The girl was already running towards the horses. She came hurrying back with the guns, Doyle's Winchester and a short-barrelled carbine of her own.

By that time, they had recognized Kelly and his wild bunch. Tyrell was with them, seemed somehow subdued.

Grimm and Bud Lynn started shooting and the line spread out, although Kelly seemed to be keeping Tyrell close by him.

Doyle and the girl crouched behind the rock and bullets ricocheted and spat dust and grit over their hunched shoulders.

146

'How did they get here?'

He shook his head, beading a man next to Bud Lynn and bringing him down with a shot through the chest. The man's frightened horse swerved into the rider next to him and there was a tangle. The girl, on one knee, fired three swift shots, working the lever so fast that the first ejected shell case hadn't hit the ground before the sound of the third shot. Man and horse went down in a thrashing tangle, scattering the others.

Doyle stared at her.

'Father taught me to shoot when I was just a child,' she said, leading a man a foot and triggering. The lead splashed gravel just in front of his feet and he dived over a fallen log.

Doyle ducked as a bullet clipped his hatbrim, sprawled and shot while lying on his belly around the base of the rock. But there were no targets now. The men had found cover and Ace Kelly bawled:

'Give it up, Doyle! You see these boulders up here? They ain't deep in the ground. One man can move 'em easy. There're four of us here so we won't have no trouble . . . Toss out your guns and stand on that big rock with your hands up . . . Or we'll push the mountain down on you!'

'You'd block the entrance completely!' Doyle called back. 'You'd never get in then!'

'Sounds like it's possible now, though, huh?' Kelly said with a laugh, pleased that he'd made Doyle betray that much information, even if indirectly. 'Wondered what shape it'd be in after that explosion.'

'We can make a run for the entrance!' Claire said, already gathering herself for the move.

Doyle didn't argue; it would be better than trusting Kelly not to shoot them in cold blood. He levered a fresh shell into the rifle's breech and nodded. 'Let's go!'

It was only a matter of fifty yards but it was uphill and they zigzagged, Doyle dropping well behind the girl because of the splinter wound in his side. The men above started shooting. Bullets *phutttedd* into the ground around his pounding boots. The girl made the entrance – then lunged back, grabbed his left arm which was flailing out to the side so as to balance the rifle and literally dragged him into the shelter of the rock overhanging the mine entrance.

Panting, gasping, they sprawled headlong, then as the shooting outside stopped, they forced themselves to their feet and staggered into the darkness, tasting dust still, smelling something like mud in a stagnant pool.

Methane – otherwise known as marsh gas, thought Doyle, hoping they weren't going to suffocate . . . .

Outside, they could hear Kelly shouting and cussing, and then the whinnying of horses and the thud of hoofs. They certainly weren't giving up the chase!

Doyle turned to speak with the girl but she was already groping her way deeper into the hillside, calling her father. He swore, then saw the first of the killers. A man stretched out low along his horse's back and charged at the entrance. Doyle, crouching by the first corner in the tunnel, coughing, fired, missing, the bullet ricocheting wildly from one wall. The rider threw himself off the horse and Doyle held his fire as he recognized Cash Tyrell.

The man scrambled towards him on all fours, yelling his name. Bullets crashed through the entrance and whined around the tunnel, causing Doyle to duck even as Tyrell fell sprawling almost at his feet.

'Gimme a gun!' the man gasped, reaching for Doyle's Colt. 'We can take 'em between us!'

Doyle slapped his hand aside roughly, using the hot barrel of his rifle. Tyrell swore and nursed his wrist and in the vague light washing this far into the tunnel, Doyle saw that the man had been badly beaten.

'No gun, Cash! Stay if you want, but no gun!'

Tyrell's horse was snorting, rolling its eyes, not liking it inside the mine. Guns crashed from outside and the animal reared and whinnied, hoofs scraping the roof. Then it stumbled out, still snorting, limping.

'C'mon!'

Doyle pushed Tyrell ahead of him, towards the fading sound of the girl as she still called her father. Then her voice grew stronger as if she had turned her face towards them to shout down the tunnel.

'I can hear him! There's a lot of rubble – he's trapped somewhere behind . . .' The word cut off short and Doyle thought he heard a sob.

He shoved Tyrell impatiently, hearing Kelly and his men coming into the entrance, back around a corner of the tunnel. The light was even dimmer here and he glimpsed the girl down on her knees, scrabbling at the wall of rock and old, splintered timbers and earth that had fallen in the explosion. He thought she was trying desperately to dig towards her father, but then he saw that what she was trying to get out from under the pile of rubble was the distorted shape ot the almost flattened squirrel's cage.

'He's dead! He must be dead!' she choked and Doyle, watching Tyrell out of the corner of his eye, placed a hand on her shoulder.

'I'm sorry, Claire. But the important thing now is to get your father out – and Kelly and his men are coming fast.'

She must have heard the clatter of rocks and the distorted voices as the killers cursed when they fell while groping their way into the tunnel.

'The debris doesn't seem to reach to the roof,' Cash Tyrell said suddenly, panting. He had climbed part-way up the sloping wall of earth. 'We can dig enough away to slide through.'

Doyle handed his rifle to the girl, clambered up beside Tyrell who was already scooping dirt aside with both hands, dropped to his knees and started doing the same. It was loose, came easily. Doyle called Doc Dawson's name and there was a faint reply from the pitch darkness beyond.

'Claire! Up here!' Doyle called urgently. 'You can squeeze through!'

The girl made her way up awkwardly and Doyle slid aside, helping her into the hole he and Tyrell had scooped away. It was only when she forced herself inside the other part of the tunnel that he realized she hadn't been holding the rifles. He spun around and felt the muzzle of a gun prod his sore ribs. Tyrell bared his teeth.

'I've got the carbine, Matt! She dropped your rifle durin' the climb! Come on! Get through! We're in this together now!'

'I thought we were in it together at the shack – just before you shot me and burned the place down around me!'

Their ears bent with the thunder of gunfire as Kelly and Grimm and the others started shooting as they rounded the corner. The bullets punched into the soil around their legs and boots and Tyrell dived for the hole, squirming and writhing to force his body through. Doyle lunged after him as guns crashed behind him again and rolled down the slope on the far side. He cannoned into Tyrell who was kneeling at the foot of the slope, working the lever on the carbine.

'Block the damn hole, you fool!' the man snapped and Doyle, groping about to do just that, felt the end of a splintered, squared support beam.

'Lend a hand!' gritted Doyle, ducking as a bullet kicked dirt into his face.

One thing about Tyrell, if he felt he was personally in danger he didn't waste time. He was beside Doyle in a moment and together they hauled the heavy timber up to the hole they had scooped out and rammed it into the space. They heard lead thunk into the wood, pushed the splintered end through to the other tunnel and then rolled and slid down the slope.

The girl was nowhere to be seen. In fact, they couldn't see much of anything: there was very little light coming through. Kelly's voice reached them, ranting at his men to get that damn log or whatever the hell it was cleared away – and *pronto*!

'Claire?'

'Here!' She answered Doyle's call, her voice sounding quite a ways off. 'There's another bend. Father's

151

got one leg trapped! Help me . . .'

Doyle groped his way towards her voice, hearing Tyrell following. He didn't know how Kelly was doing but with three or four of them pushing they would likely move the beam in a matter of minutes.

He had to use those minutes to the best advantage.

'Who's that with you, Matt?' Doc Dawson gritted as Tyrell came up. 'Oh, Lord! It would have to be you, Cash!'

'We can get you out,' Tyrell said as Doyle and the girl struggled to find what was pinning Dawson's left leg. 'The hell happened?'

Doc laughed briefly, bitterly. 'Shared a cell with an old miner, Mort Thoms. He helped me dig the escape tunnel under the wall. Told me about old mines and accumulated gas. Said it was usually in pockets. To save time, the old-timers would take a candle, smash away the tallow with a gun butt, and expose several inches of wick. They'd light this in a place they knew had clean air, toss it around the next bend in the tunnel. If there was a pool of bad gas there it usually went up with flash and a bang, but burned away. Like a fool, I tried it. Must've been one helluva big pool because it like to've tore the mountain down!'

'You killed Tonto!' Claire said, unable to keep bitter accusation out of her voice. 'I found his cage, crushed.'

They were digging while talking and Dawson's voice was a lot softer when he said, 'He wasn't in it, Claire – I tried using him to test the gas but when I saw how – distressed it made him, I took him outside into the fresh air and let him into the woods. I figured you'd like it best that way.'

She was silent, then sobbed and reached up to hug him.

'Quit that!' gasped Tyrell. 'His leg's almost free now. Matt, lend a hand to lift this rock off him.'

The girl scraped more dirt away from the rock while the men strained and then it came up a few inches and with a wrenching grunt, Doc Dawson pulled his leg free and rolled away onto his side.

There were sounds that told them Kelly and his men were about to break through.

'I'm comin' for you, Doc!' Kelly yelled, voice distorted and booming in the tunnel. 'And you better have that iron box ready for me, you double-crossin' son of a bitch!'

'Help me up!' gritted Dawson, reaching out towards Tyrell, who stepped out of reach, brought the carbine around, menacing.

'Just where *is* the box, Doc?'

'Somewhere under all this rubble,' Dawson snapped. 'It's gone! Now let's get out of here. No use dying for nothing.'

'You're lyin'!' growled Tyrell.

'OK. You stay and start digging! Matt? Claire?'

They grabbed Doc's arms and lifted him, hearing the rattle of stones and rubble as Kelly and his men made their way through the tunnel, approaching the bend. Dawson was unsteady on his feet, dragging at them, but they limped their way into the darkness.

Tyrell hesitated, then fired a shot back at the tunnel bend. There was a spark as the lead struck some protruding rock and the ricochet's whine repeated itself twice more as it zigzagged from one side of the tunnel to the other. They heard Kelly and his men yelling, no doubt dropping flat in an effort to escape the runaway bullet. Tyrell triggered two more shots and hurried after the others.

'If you're lyin', Doc . . .!' he gritted but there was no answer.

'Is there any way out of here?' Doyle gasped and Doc Dawson surprised him by saying:

'Right around the next bend. I found it earlier, came back and tossed that burning candle, thinking to seal the tunnel in case – someone came after me.'

Doyle hesitated but Dawson shoved against him.

'Keep going!'

'I see it!' Claire said suddenly. 'There's a glow up ahead!'

'Wait a minute!' Tyrell snapped suddenly behind them and Doyle heard the lever of the carbine work once more. 'You said you came *back*! You wouldn't seal the tunnel if you hadn't already found the box!'

Doc Dawson, hopping on his good leg, shoved Claire down hard, drawing a gasp of surprise from her. He spun towards Doyle.

'Get him, Matt!'

Doc had detected the savage anger in Tyrell's voice and knew the man would fire indiscriminately in uncontrolled fury – and he was right. The carbine crashed and Dawson went down, air slammed from him by the force of a bullet-strike.

Doyle dropped to one knee, palming up his sixgun. The carbine lever was just clashing home when he triggered two fast shots.

Cash Tyrell spun wildly, the carbine firing into the

154

broken ground as he fell. He lay on one elbow trying to work the lever once more. Doyle shot him again.

And at the same time Kelly, Grimm and a third man came stumbling around the bend, all shooting. Bullets swarmed like wasps through the tunnel, gouging lines of dirt from the walls and roof, striking sparks from quartz outcrops, buzzing wildly. Doyle yelled at Claire to get down but she was already lying prone, shaking her father.

'Keep – going,' he gasped. 'We're almost – there.'

Doyle knew they were silhouetted now against the light spilling in from the distant exit hole. Kelly and his men started shooting again and he felt the passage of a bullet past his face. Crouched double, dragging Dawson between them, they made for the exit hole. Doc was biting back gasps of pain but they kept going, Doyle shooting one-handed. He thought he heard a man gag back there.

'You won't make it, Doc!' yelled Kelly. 'You're too – late.'

But Doyle and the girl were already pushing and thrusting the wounded Dawson through into the sunlight and Matt grabbed Claire, heaving her through bodily. He crouched, reloading, hearing the others running now that they could see a little better.

He only had three bullets in the chambers; he snapped the cylinder closed and dropped flat as he emptied the gun into the running men. Grimm staggered and fell to one knee, blood coursing down his face. Kelly ran into him and somersaulted over the downed man.

Doyle rolled free into the sunlight and slid down a

small slope of soft earth. Dawson, grimed and bloody, was pointing to a rock balanced over the exit hole.

'Close it!' he croaked and Doyle lunged up, clambered up to the rock and put his shoulder against it. He saw that the boulder had been wedged in precariously with smaller rocks. He kicked them free and almost fell as it dropped over the edge, his side wet with new blood.

'*Now* it's time for reckonin', Doc!' Kelly yelled as he struggled through the exit hole.

He was half-way through when the boulder came down on him. Claire covered her scarred face with her hands as the killer was crushed . . . and the hole was sealed.

They helped Dawson down the slope and into a small arroyo. But when Doyle started to heave him across his shoulders Doc shook his head.

'Wait. Over there – under that bush . . . I – I pulled it out and dropped the box into the hole, before I went back to seal the tunnel.' He tried to grin but the pain turned it into a grimace. 'Cash was right – I found the box first.'

Doyle looked at him, and handed his sixgun to the girl, unbuckling his cartridge belt and tossing it to her.

'Reload for me, Claire.'

She frowned but commenced the reloading as he moved to the bush, pulled it out of the ground and saw the iron cube of the express box, half-concealed by dirt. He heaved it up, amazed at its weight, and dragged it across to where the girl and the wounded Dawson waited.

Then Doc snatched the partly reloaded Colt from

Claire, snapped the cylinder closed and cocked the hammer in his blood-slippery hands, covering Doyle.

'Father!' the girl gasped, trying to grab the gun but he thrust her away, face contorting again with the effort.

'Just drag it over here, Matt, then you can carry it back to where the horses are. You'll need both hands so I'll look after your gun.'

Doyle glared and then hefted the box in both hands, muscles bulging in his arms.

'Gimme your arm, Claire, and let's go' Dawson said. The girl hesitated, but then obeyed, supporting her father, Doyle walking out front, struggling under the weight of the iron box. The girl helped her father along behind as they made their way around the mountain to where the horses waited.

'Sorry about turning your gun on you, Matt, but I can't take any chances from here on in.'

Doyle smiled faintly at the fugitive as the girl finished binding the wound in the man's side. The one in his thigh – on the leg that had been trapped by the rockfall – had bled a lot because the bullet had passed clear through the fleshy part of the upper thigh. It was painful but not incapacitating.

'Doc, I can't remember whenever you *did* take a chance.'

Pale and drawn beneath the dirt smearing his face, Dawson managed to smile.

'That's why I'm here now.'

'I guess that's right. What now? You gonna have Claire tie me up again so you can ride off into the sunset?'

157

Claire glanced at Doyle sharply and then turned to her father.

'What is going to happen now, father?'

'That damn box is a problem. I've got to get it open somehow. I'm sure the coins and dies are in there, just by the weight and shaking it . . .'

'And once you do have it open?' the girl persisted.

Dawson sobered. 'Then, Claire, my dear, you and I are taking a long journey – to South America, just as planned.'

Her eyes flicked across Doyle's face as she asked,

'Are we going to stay there – for ever?'

Dawson drew down a deep breath, pressed a hand against his throbbing side, shook his head slowly. 'You won't have to. You'll be able to come back anytime you want.'

She frowned. 'If you're wanted and I run with you, I'll be on the wanted list, too. They'll soon recognize me with . . .' She touched the scarred side of her face.

Dawson smiled slowly.

'Not necessarily. Mainly because, with a little luck, and a lot of that there gold in the iron box, those scars'll be removed over the course of a year or there-abouts. You may not look *exactly* as you did before the fire, but you'll surely have a face you won't have to hide from – anyone.' When he said this last, his gaze went to Doyle.

'Are you talking about this – special surgery?' Doyle asked, surprised to find his breath a little short.

'Plastic surgery they're calling it,' Doc replied. 'Yes, that's what I'm talking about, Matt. Claire, there's a doctor down there in Buenos Aires who is making quite a name for himself, treating burn victims, taking skin from other parts of their bodies and growing it over the scarred areas. It's not – guaranteed, but there's a good chance of success . . . and it's expensive, but now we have the iron box, the expense don't matter . . .'

Claire was shaking, her eyes wide. Then she knelt beside Dawson and threw her arms about his neck.

'All along you had planned this – for me?'

'Soon as I read about this doctor, name of Mendes, by the by. Studied in Vienna and – no matter. He *knows* what he's doing. It's up to you now to decide whether you want him to work on you or not.'

Strangely, she turned to Doyle.

'Help me decide, Matt! Please . . . ?'

He took her arm and smiled down at her. 'Well, I'd sure like to see both sides of your face looking the same, see you walking down the street – maybe on my arm – that yaller hair blowing free in the wind, those clear blue eyes meeting the stares of everyone you pass, squarely and happily . . . and proudly, Claire. That's what I'd like to see.'

Her teeth tugged gently at her lower lip.

'Would – would you wait a year? Maybe more . . . ?'

'I'd wait forever if I had to,' Doyle found himself saying. 'But it'd drive me crazy. Reckon I could stand it for a year, though, but then I'd be looking for you.'

She smiled broadly, turning her good side towards him. And he knew this is how he wanted her to look, how she *would* look next time he saw her.

Somewhere nearby a squirrel chattered in the trees.

159